DISCOVERIES

VINNIE PEACHEY

DISCOVERIES

ISBN: 978-0-578-34894-0

Cover and Interior Design by the Author.

CONTENTS:

Author's Note_____

"Landscape" _____ 1

"Plethora Beyond the Gates" _____ 26

"Crawling Rain" _____ 36

"The Risk of Worship" _____ 38

"Uprooting" _____ 57

"The Balance" _____ 63

"Mother's Petals" _____ 131

"Just Above the Chin" _____ 133

"Lone Diner" _____ 161

About the Author _____

AUTHOR'S NOTE:

While I was writing these stories (most of them), I had a routine of visiting my hometown to help with a major project. Days were spent in the mountains, cutting dead trees to the ground, creating noise, almost like a mechanical song to let the forest know we were there, to let the nearby animals know to take guard, stay away. For the time being, that is.

Then darkness would come, pushing us out, knowing our visibility (or lack of) was a safety concern. After stepping out of the woods, going back to our modernness, it was then that very same forest came alive with its own song—many songs. Animals started to move, and insects started to sing. I could hear them; I knew they were there. But where? Hiding in the black, away from us. Yet they *were*, in fact, there, confirmation of things that can be so close without being seen. It creates an uncertainty: What really is out there to be found? And this is just the surface, the woodland creatures moving on the ground and in the trees.

So…what about the things we can't observe or hear right in front of us, whether it be day or night? Items buried, lost or unwritten history, the possibility of invisible forces in our proximity, et cetera. This film of the unknown is what I tried to pierce through when writing these stories; I wanted to create these types of discoveries. In some cases, though, like what my characters encounter, perhaps it's best we don't find such things so regularly. I fear the questions and confusion after the experience could be more destructive and maddening compared to the ignorance of never knowing what's truly among us—that's been there all along—waiting unseen.

For Kristin,
the constant image of patience and affection

Special Thanks to Dan,
who reads everything I write and assisted in this book's
outcome.

And to Cathy:
You took me under your wing and inspired some stories
along the way.

DISCOVERIES

"I am in bed, and I am safe.
No matter where my dreams may take me tonight,
home again is where I will always wake."

"And so…
we melt,
revealing new skin."

"The forest changes at night.
For in the dark is where the small, crawling ones
sound so large and dominant
with their ancient yet ageless song."

"LANDSCAPE"

1.

THE WORLD WAS still hunting for the photographer known as Valurie Bide. There were some, however, that were far more interested in her than others. The law in numerous countries, for example, had been searching for Valurie for more than five years—and they had been looking for the *least* amount of time. Her followers wanted to (after all this time) put a face to the artist, for she had always covered and protected herself, hiding her identity for more than two decades. This fact alone was the reason why no one had been able to place her behind bars after all the assumptions and accusations started to pile.

Valurie had her first breakthrough in the art community in the last quarter of 1998. Even then, right out of the gate, she kept herself hidden, wanting to spark mystery from the start. She was a wonderful photographer, capturing pictures of breathtaking landscapes from across the world. In her early career, she would secretly leave behind prints of her work in front of major galleries and reputable art stores, mainly in the United States initially until lengthening this act to different countries in Europe. A letter usually accompanied the work, proclaiming that the owners of the establishment could have the prints free of charge and sell the images at the price they determined was appropriate for each. She did this countless times, in countless cities.

Galleries began communicating amongst themselves, and all of them stated how easy it was to sell such beauty. However, everyone said that the identity they had captured on their outside video security camera was entirely different from the next. In one, it definitely appeared to be a woman of average build and dressed in black. Another establishment explained that it looked to be an old man delivering a large, wrapped package. At each deposit site, it was a different person altogether captured on a camera, except their build: weighing approximately 120 pounds, around five foot three inches. People started to guess that it was the same person, just wearing disguises. Valurie would also leave a print (or more) in public places, like hotel rooms and city parks. At hotels, her registered name was always an alias. And so, the questions began: Who was Valurie Bide exactly? Why did she not want to be seen?

As Valurie's notoriety grew, the value and prestige of her work grew commensurately. Lucky was the gallery that found her work on its doorstep; luckier still were the few people who found her works in the wild.

Others would say that her work was nothing too special. Most of her photographs simply focused on a mountainous range and a sunset or sunrise. They almost seemed simple or…at least done by countless other photographers, not worth the large amounts of money people paid to get a print. Though, many, *many* did, just to say they had such a piece in their collection—a Valurie Bide piece!— claim to certain bragging rights. On the other hand, countless believed that her eye and patience was superior. The way the sunlight penetrated the wilderness was something of...adolescence, nostalgia, inspiration. One magazine even published a quote saying: "Her photographs frequently give people a certain feeling, a sensation that they've already seen the landscape somewhere before, perhaps stood at that precise location at least once in their lives, even if they wholeheartedly know they never visited such locations in the world." She was able to find these beautiful openings where the sun would rise or fall ideally, creating a spectrum of colors before hiding behind the mountains. The contrast of colors in the sky against the greens and yellows of nature was almost mesmerizing, hypnotic. Photographers alike imagined the patience, the hours that had to be spent in a single place to get such perfect pictures, the right adjustment of colors, and that intense divergence of hues.

No one knew exactly where her photographs were taken; she labeled and titled them all terribly vaguely. If the picture had been taken in Washington state in say...1998, the title on the back of the print would read "Washington 1998." If it had been taken in Spain 2008, it would read "Spain 2008." There were never cities listed, only states or countries.

Valurie had hundreds to her catalog, and eventually she or someone else had built a website where people not-so-lucky to buy or find one in the wild could purchase a print of their choosing, going all the way back to her original breakthrough photographs. However, and oddly, her website was only live and accessible during the winter months. When she came out of social hiding each year, it was known then that she was still alive, still at work. Rumors started that she did not travel during such times of the year and was able to manage her website then, alone, privately, printing and sending out her work on her own in secret, from an unknown location. Her social-media platforms were a shadow of her website—only active during the winter, listing old photographs of her work that were now (for the time being) for sale online. The return labels on her packages were always blank, the postmarks were always stamped in different cities, and a disguise had been worn at every mail deposit box, as told by ones who saw the video footage. She was a master at many things, especially keeping her face hidden.

But why? That was what so many people wondered. Was that her game? Her...way to sell herself? Continue to stay a mystery, let people say your name instead of having to do it yourself? Regardless of her reasoning, her net worth grew with each given year, the longer the mystery had life. And just as mysteriously, some of her photographs even had a constant signature, a repeating item, which caused quite a stir and a torrent of rumors in the community. What was the meaning of this—this shovel and a bow?

By 2015, seventeen years since her debut, there were fifty-eight photographs with a shovel pierced in the ground, often with a red or pink Christmas-like bow near the top of the handle. This was her signature, denoting an indisputable Valurie Bide piece. People started to say it was a treasure hunt, claiming that since there was a shovel in the pictures, then something had to be buried nearby these locations. Or perhaps something was left behind, waiting to be found. Money? Another photograph of value? It became a sort of game, with nearly a cult-like following. Over the years, people testified they had found such locations, some even trying to recreate a scene with their own cameras. But no actual evidence was ever shown, just hearsay, wannabe wishes, and untouchable fantasies, only being able to come so close to such glory through falsification.

With her titles being so vague, it was nearly impossible to guess where this shovel or prize could be unless one really knew the area or randomly stumbled upon such an item in the thick of the unknown. But...good luck. If no one knew who she was, it was assumed that these shovels would also never be found, located with such care and isolation as herself.

Some people are just plain lucky, though.

And other people, their fortune grows in the most unethical ways.

2.

ON AUGUST 8TH, 2015, London Young, recently single, registered nurse, age thirty, slowly drove as he searched for his next Airbnb location to rest for the evening. He pulled onto a quarter-mile long stone driveway in northern Iceland that led to a small horse farm higher up on the property, easily visible in the vast openness. The name of the lane was impossible to say; it was approximately eighteen characters long and there were too many consonants beside one another. Fences were on either side of the vehicle, some containing horses, others held sheep. It was day four of his travels around the island and it was getting dark as he shut off the motor to his 4x4 rental. The house next to him was modest for a farm home. He could see under the glow of the patio light that there were at least ten pairs of shoes and boots outside the door, most covered in mud or shit. The smell of shit was close, too. The grass was high in the yard near the stone driveway, and there were goats and chickens filtering through the green, organically trimming it. A collie dog came racing out of one of the barns, eager to greet the stranger. A ripped soccer ball hung in its mouth.

The door to the house opened and a woman of probably twenty-five appeared. She was barely five feet in height, and her hair was wet and naturally curly, looking as though she had just emerged from the shower. It was easy to see she was not wearing a bra—her presumed size C breasts shaped the front of the long-sleeved shirt, her nipples erect and obvious. Her legs were covered by a pair of baggy sweatpants. This was not who London had made his reservation with, yet...he was not unhappy at the sight to say the least.

"You must be London," the woman said after London opened and closed the driver's door.

He smiled and brought his hand up, gesturing a distant hello. "London. Yes. That's me." He put his hand down and watched as the woman started towards him. He could not help but notice the way her breasts moved under her shirt, even in dim light. *Eyes up*, he told himself. Deep down, though, he wished for her to want him in some way, sexually if possible.

His vacation was deserved, yet possibly a reckless attempt to forget about the blindsiding end of his five-year relationship. Before Iceland, he had spent five days in Ireland. The first day he took a bus trip to see the cliffs, but after that, he had spent most of his time walking drunk around Dublin, hoping to find someone to take home to his place of rest. He struck out every evening, some nights harder than the others, depending on how fast the room was spinning, how un-hard he knew his penis would get with too much whiskey. He knew damn well not to pursue anything with parts unusable, only to find embarrassment. But this tour around Iceland, this could be different. Since he was driving, exploring the country, alcohol could not be involved, at least not during exploration hours.

"Do you need any help?" the woman asked as she came within ten feet of London.

He could smell peppermint on her. "No, I'm okay. Just the one bag for now. Thank you, though..."

"Lana," the woman replied. "My name's Lana."

London smiled at her, shouldering his bag. "Nice to meet you. You're staying here this evening I take it?"

"Tonight, and tomorrow night, too, before moving on. My boyfriend—

(Shit, London immediately thought.)

—is flying in to meet up with me the day after tomorrow. Spending a few more days here in Iceland before heading back to the airport and then off to Germany. You in the country much longer?"

"I'll be staying here overnight at this house for two days as well. Using this spot for a central point to rest for a day. Take a break from all the driving. And I'm here for about another week. I'm traveling the Ring Road."

"Oh!" Lana said. "Why don't you come with me tomorrow then if you don't have much planned? I'm headed about an hour north of here to do some hiking. I fear it will be a tourist trap but I'm sure it will be a decent enough day. Several trails to explore, waterfalls. Typical, but I got to kill a day. And I'll drive us. Give you a break."

London hummed. "Okay. Yeah. I'll accompany you tomorrow. Sounds fun."

She smiled at him.

"So where are Elda and Merle?" London asked, referring to the Airbnb hosts, the owners of the house and farm.

"Oh, of course. They left about a half hour ago to get a few grocery items for the dinner this evening. They said they'd be back later. They informed me that you may be arriving before their return. That's how I knew your name."

London nodded.

"Come," Lana said, "I'll show you to your room and around the house."

Unfortunately, London knew his bed would not be with her. In fact, he slept a floor above her, fantasizing how she would come to his door in the middle of the night, crawl in bed with him, and he would let her start to erase the memories of the past five years.

But she did not come....

3.

LONDON WOKE. HE was covered in a wool blanket, the wool apparently acquired from several sheep that once lived on the property years ago, woven by a former guest that stayed with them. It was eight in the morning, and he knew that Lana wanted to leave by nine.

Better move, he thought and sat up, searching for his luggage. He opened it and gathered the day's clothing: a flannel, jeans, and a sweatshirt. If needed, a heftier coat, hat, and raingear were in the car. He ran his fingers through is hair, then flattened it, accepting how the early-morning folds rested in the mirror.

He came down for breakfast, making sure all the crust from his eyes had been removed as he stepped down the stairs. He could smell food, something cooking or already prepared.

"Good morning, London," Elda said. A lingering yawn fell out of her mouth before she took another drink from her coffee cup.

London had finally met his hosts after he and Lana had taken a small adventure down the property into an adjacent field where she thought she had seen wild blueberries earlier that day. They had taken horses down, slow and steady, for London had always had a fear of horses—or anything bigger than him, for that matter. Lana had confidently led the way, assisting when sensing (or seeing) a discomfort in London's expressions. While the horses were tied to a fence post, they filtered through the field and gathered berries, trading stories about their hometowns, hobbies, and life. After returning, it was then that London had met Elda and Merle, each near the height of six feet and both with beautiful, natural bleach-blonde hair. Elda was the talker of the two, and London did not see much of Merle that evening, for he merely introduced himself, ate dinner with them, apologized for being tired, grabbed a magazine on his way through the living room, and went to sleep. Just as shy, he was not there in the kitchen that morning.

"Good morning. No Merle to join us?"

Elda shook her head. "He works early. Left already. Poor fella probably only got a few hours of sleep. He doesn't sleep so well, regardless how early he turns in."

London gave her a wrinkled expression. "Too bad."

"Please," Elda started, "help yourself to some coffee. A fresh pot is ready over on the counter." She pointed and sipped her mug. "Lana should be finished soon with our pancakes."

Lana turned around from the stove and smiled at London. "Good morning," she said.

London grinned. "Good morning to you, too." He grabbed a cup near the coffee pot and poured himself some. He lightly blew over his mug before taking the first swallow. "Using the blueberries like you said?"

"Sure am," Lana replied. "Have a seat. These shouldn't take but another minute. Nothing better than blueberry pancakes, but I have a feeling these are going to be the best with these wild, Icelandic ones."

And both London and Elda could not argue after their plates were cleared, their mouths containing a lingering taste of batter and sweetness, stifled only by the bitterness of coffee.

4.

"I'LL SEE YOU both later tonight. Come back hungry," Elda said to London and Lana as they jumped into Lana's rental. She waved and went back into the house, preparing for her day of cleaning up after the horses in one of the barns.

A little after an hour of travel, and London trying desperately to enjoy the terrible audio book that Lana had playing, they parked in a stone parking lot, crowded with people and at least a hundred other cars and bigger vehicles. Given the choice over again, London would have rather sat in silence during the entire ride instead of listening to the digital voice in the car, taking him on a journey of medieval knights and ridiculous creatures that roamed the mountains, surviving only in the minds of idiots. Albeit, it appeared that Lana was fully engaged to the story, especially since she did not say but a mouthful of words to London the entire trip, so London, respectfully, did not ask to turn it off. London was not much of a reader or one for the arts in general, music being his greatest interest in the realm, and even then, his library was limited to modern rock and roll and nostalgic songs from when he was in high school, the ones he thought would never be famous but now often heard on the radio. As far as literature, he had trouble with fiction, trying to accept scenarios and landscapes that could not be easily found around him or on a computer screen. Seeing things for the reality they were was easier, trustworthy, and took less thinking, less time. He could not argue, though, that with another voice around him, telling him a story, there was no time to think of the heartache that was still inside him. This fiction, for the time being, was a mild sedative for his painful existence. And for that, he was more thankful for the stranger's voice than its initial annoyance. But the narrator was gone now since the power of the vehicle was off, and London hoped that Lana and this hike would be enough to smother old memories from coming to surface.

"I figured there would be a lot of people here," Lana confessed. "Hopefully I can still get some good shots without too many bodies." She went to the hatch of her rental, opening it. There she opened a small duffle bag, retrieving (what looked to be) an expensive camera. She put it around her neck, grabbed her day bag, and closed the hatch.

"You did say yesterday while we were picking the blueberries that you liked to take photographs."

"Iceland has such beauty to capture. Don't you think?"

London nodded. "Very much so."

Together, they started behind the rows of people, following them up the initial hiking trail cutout of the cliff-side. To their right was another mountainous cliff made of volcanic rock. A river or large stream created by a glacier runoff separated the two cliffs. There was a waterfall further out, continuously feeding and cycling the river. A helicopter flew overhead. London had assumed a visual tour of the area, but it quickly went out of sight, its rotating propellers no longer audible.

"Or someone's vehicle got stuck and they called for rescue," Lana continued.

London raised his eyebrows. "Yes, or that."

After nearly half a mile, London and Lana had options. The trail quickly turned into a nervous system of other trails to take, leading further up the cliff's height.

"Take your pick," London said. "Where do you think you will find the best pictures to take?"

Lana hummed and picked the one with the least amount of people. London was not surprised.

The choice seemed to be the correct one, for Lana could not take but a few steps without stopping, focusing her shot, snapping a photo. London would often go out ahead of her, pointing and showing her locations just ahead of them that could be worth the capture—or so he thought.

He was trying to involve himself, show her interest, even if this was supposed to be his day of rest, even if she had a boyfriend.

At the highest point of the trail, they stopped, finding a small cave in which to have a quick lunch. Only a couple of hikers came by, saw them eating, and went on their way. Lana had prepared a spread of fruit, vegetables, nuts, and jerky of some kind the night before. After finishing, they both agreed that they wished there would be a bathroom around of some kind, their remaining morning coffee needing an escape.

"I think I can find a place here in the cave to use," Lana said. "I don't think I'll be bothered."

"You want me to wait?"

"No, you go and find your own spot. I gotta go now."

"All right. I'm going to go and find a tree nearby. I'll keep my eye on the cave entrance and yell at anyone that gets too close."

"My hero," Lana chuckled.

London left and jogged up the embankment, perching just above the cave entrance. He could see people down in the distance walking on different trails of the cliff. And just in view from their location was the parking lot. They had to be miles away. He turned and found the closest trees he could find, skinny pines that did not provide much cover at all. Fearing that someone may see him exposed, he turned away from the distant people, turning away from the cave entrance, going back on his word so someone would not see him and his member.

He quickly zipped himself up when he heard

footsteps. When he turned, there was Lana no more than ten feet away from him.

"Jesus," London started. "You scared me. I heard someone but didn't expect you. I was about to come back down. Guess we should get back on the trail."

"Don't be scared of me," she said and threw herself at him, locking her lips on him, her tongue meeting his.

Though in complete shock, London accepted and participated in the utter surprise.

They parted, hearts racing.

"But your boyfriend..." London said.

She shook her head. "No boyfriend. Only a lie to protect myself from men I don't know. Eliminates them trying from the start. Allows me to pick and choose who I like. And I like you."

"Fair enough."

He went to kiss her again, but she stopped him. London looked at her, confused.

"Not here," she started. "Let's get further away from people. Get off this trail and be hidden, even if the signs say not to stray from the path."

And so, they did, Lana leading London up and over the highest point they could find, shielding themselves from the ones on the other side of the peak. They fell to the ground on an open patch of moss, the river's song down below them somewhere. There were hardly any trees here, only similar saplings that London used as a bathroom. They were in the open, barely hidden.

Lana was on top of London, undoing his pants. He helped her, sliding them down. Lana fell to the side of him, undoing her own. She looked at him.

"Do you want me?" she asked.

"Since I've laid my eyes on you," London confessed.

She smiled and moved back towards him, grabbing
at his groin. She turned and faced the opposite direction and
started to sit on him.

"Dear God," Lana said at first as he slid into her.

A warmth smothered London's crotch.

"I know, right?"

But that was it: one quick penetration. She quickly
got up and off London. She stood there, her buttocks above
him nearly glowing like twin moons.

"I thought you wanted me?" London questioned.

"I do. Just...just wait."

"What's the problem now? It was just happening.
Tease much?"

"I'm sorry. I'll make this up to you. I promise. Let
me explain." She started to put on her pants. "London, do
you know of a photographer by the name of Valurie Bide?"

London laid there and thought to himself, his penis
softening, curling downward like a sad trunk. "I don't think
I know of *any* photographers." He reached to his ankles,
feeling for the waistband of his jeans.

Lana opened her backpack and got her phone.
"Come on, come on," she said after typing "Valurie Bide
Iceland Photograph" in the search engine—knowing damn
well she would have to use a search engine to see Valurie's
pictures instead of going directly to one of her social media
platforms. Lana knew those were down and only accessible
in the winter. She was familiar with the artist and her ways.
"Come on. Load already."

"Who's this photographer you speak of? And why now?"

Quickly, Lana gave London a brief history of the photographer: how no one knew who she was, how she secretly produced most of her works, how there were specific photographs that people hunt for and have never found. Her thumb was swiping her phone now, searching.

"Yes!" Lana screamed.

London sat up. She came to him, sitting beside him, shoving her phone into his vision.

"See?" Lana asked. "We're sitting in this very spot."

London looked at the phone and then ahead of him. The landscape was in a great decline, the mossy earth and small saplings transitioning into full, thick trees closer to the river. On the opposite side of the stream were more trees, climbing higher and higher up the incline of the opposing cliff. The cliffs made this organic "M" shape against the sky. In the photo, the sky was a mixture of pinks and purples; before London and Lana, the sky was a sheet of smooth blue. But it did look like the same place. There was one obvious difference, though.

"I don't see a shovel down by where the trees start," London said. "But it really does look like the same place."

"It *is* the same place. I know it. Maybe the shovel is just missing, or...the weather took it down. The caption of the picture says that it was taken nearly eight years ago." Lana started down the cliffside.

"Where are you going?"

"Are you kidding? To see if this is really the spot. Her followers die for this opportunity we have. I know you probably don't get it, but...but this is a huge thing we are about to experience if this, indeed, is the correct spot. And I know it is. That river, and the shape of the cliffs against the sky. I bet there is an old shovel down there if we search hard enough." She turned again, and London knew she was doing this with or without him, with or without London being able to understand as to why something like this even stopped sex. But it did, and for that, what they had stumbled upon must be priceless to the right person. He stood and followed her.

There was no shovel in the area. Lana even got on her hands and knees, digging at the earth, trying to locate the spade where it appeared to rest in the photo. But it was hard to tell exactly from the perspective of the photograph and the reality where they stood. She thought she was close, though.

"Take a break. Why don't you look for a handle or something nearby? I'll look around for the spade. Maybe some wind or rain or snow knocked it over at one point or another and it broke, moved it away from the exact spot."

Lana got up, exhausted from her excited digging. "Okay. Maybe you're right. I have to use the bathroom again anyway. Gonna go into the trees there a bit. You search the grounds here for that spade. On my way out, I'll look for a handle of some kind."

London nodded and bent down.

Before she entered the trees, Lana turned back to London. "I'm sorry, you know? I'll make it up to you. We have the rest of the day, not to mention a remaining night in the same house. I still want you."

"I hope so," London admitted as he watched her

enter the thick of trees.

London could not find the energy to dig into the ground. His mind was elsewhere. Lana still wanted him, and the thought of continuing where they had left off kept his mind away from Lana's request to keep digging, to find the spade.

A scream broke London's sexual vision immediately. He got to his feet and bolted to where he saw Lana disappear. This was questionably the bravest thing he had done, yet he did not process it then, only acted naturally, primally.

London slid to a stop when he saw Lana knelt in a random area of forest. Without touching her, he could tell she was shaking. She was sniffling, too. He bent behind her, looking over her shoulder. She was holding the bones of a human hand. London's heart sank. He felt as if he were to be sick, but he swallowed confidently.

"It's a hand," Lana wept.

"I know it is," London replied. "But whose?"

5.

BY THAT EVENING, London and Lana's discovery was global news. Not only was a hand discovered, but an entire human skeleton below the earth's surface. It appeared to be buried, purposely at that. Lana had explained to reporters that she had recognized the landscape and knew it was the location of a Valurie Bide photograph and pursued, regardless if it was recklessly off the trail and advised against. They could have been hurt or lost, ending up like the bones they had found. And it was lucky that this body was found to begin with. The grounds here were slowly descending with the overflow from the melting glacier. The river could not hold the runoff and had created a system of smaller streams in various areas. Roots of trees were showing here, and with the deterioration of earth, slowly, the grave moved close to the earth's surface and eventually a reaching hand poked through, as if they were trying to claw their way out before all air had been lost. There were old ropes and tape in the grave with the bones, assumed to be the devices to restrain this individual. Upon further investigation of the grounds, not only was a body found, but the blade of a shovel and broken handle. Immediately, this started a slew of questions: Did Valurie Bide kill this person? Was that the clue of the shovel in the photographs? Were there more bodies to be found?

World officials got most of their help from the media, reaching out to the art community, asking people to come forward if they knew of any exact locations of Valurie Bide's photographs, specifically and more importantly the ones containing a shovel. Out of all the photos with shovels in them, more than ten countries would be involved in the search for these secret locations.

The hand the Lana found belonged to a man who had gone missing in Iceland almost eight years ago. His car was found unlocked and abandoned in the same stone parking lot where Lana and London had parked that day. After looking up the name Valurie Bide, it was a disappointment to officials to see that no one by such name had even visited the country, nor was there ever a passport made and issued to that name. It was then announced that Valurie Bide was a pseudonym and not her real identity.

It was not much of a surprise to her followers, though, since videos of her were never the same, always a different persona. However, what did shock a lot of people was what one person, an old, retired police detective named Oliver from a small town in Pennsylvania, oddly discovered once it was known to the world that Valurie's name was not her real name.

6.

OLIVER LOVED HIS puzzles—puzzles in the morning paper, crosswords, word searches, ones where you had to unscramble several words to get a correct phrase or sentence. He did them during breakfast, the news, even while sitting with his daily friends at the local pub.

While sitting in his recliner watching the evening news, Oliver was yet again in the middle of one of his puzzles. This one was mindless, a simple word search, yet it kept him more entertained than the constant heartache on the television. But after so much, it is nearly impossible to look away, not to listen, especially since the world was still looking for Valurie Bide, and the story was getting coverage on news stations several times a day.

Being a retired detective, this story about Valurie Bide haunted him. He could not do much about it since being off the force, but he was…still programmed, wanting to help. But what could he do just sitting there, doing puzzles all day?

In a column beside his current wordsearch, he quickly wrote down "Valurie Bide." He focused on it, and even though he and everyone else knew her name was an alias, he still questioning whether he had ever seen the name Valurie spelled that way. He stared more and it seemed the letters of her name started to move, changing, rearranging themselves. The rearrangement was automatic, stemming from work on certain puzzles, old duties on the force, and a bizarre instance a few years ago when he deciphered another individual's name—an odd gentleman that visited his local pub just once—only to find his name was an anagram for the phrase "Hail Satan." Now, was this person really the Devil? Doubtful, but certain information was never found, and everyone that witnessed the dancing flame on the car had no explanation other than the supernatural. Oliver's mind refocused on Valurie, considering. Could Valurie Bide be an anagram, too? Could he find, create other words with the letters of her name? His eyes returned to his page, absorbed. He began to write down a variety of words that he saw within her name. And a moment later, his eyes widened. He had found something, something that was too precise to be a coincidence, too close to what had been dug up and discovered in Iceland.

"I'll be damned," he said.

As quickly as he could, he went for the phone and called his dear friend who still worked for the local police.

"Chuck, listen to me now. That Valurie Bide photographer that everyone is looking for…"

"Yeah?" Chuck replied.

"Her name isn't just an alias!" Oliver yelled into the phone. "Valurie Bide is an anagram! If you rearrange the letters of her name, it creates the grisly phrase 'buried alive.' She has to be the one responsible for that fella they found in Iceland. *Has* to be. I'm telling you! It's too much of a coincidence. Tell everyone you can."

Word spread quickly after Oliver's discovery circulated throughout the states, then the world, which only put pressure on officials from around the globe to find more of these locations since it appeared that the person that London and Lana had found had been, in fact, buried alive. And so, more help was asked for from her followers.

Within two months, fifteen of Valurie's locations were found in seven different countries, all of which contained human remains, all buried beneath the earth's surface. There were many more to locate and stack to Valurie's charge of murders. Her being outed as one of the most disgusting and successful serial killers only made her following grow, only made people want to know who she was, to see the face capable of doing these things.

But still, no one could find her after the bodies started to be removed from the ground. She had deleted herself from the media—her website was down, all social media platforms were deleted and deactivated. She had been caught and many believed it was fear that caused her to go into complete hiding for over five years. In that time, thirty of her locations were discovered, along with the bodies. Some were still to be found, unknown locations to all but the artist.

7.

ON SEPTEMBER 2ND, 2020, Stewart Hess turned on his blinker and slowly made his way to the highway rest stop. He needed a bathroom and a coffee, maybe even a snack before getting to his hotel for the evening, which was at least another hour, just over the Colorado border. When he got back to his car, he sat there, softly singing along with the radio, waiting for his terrible vending-machine coffee to cool. A bag of M&M's laid on the seat beside him, recently purchased but unopened.

A terrible metallic bang echoed against his window, causing him to jerk, spilling a splash of hot coffee on his lap.

"Dammit!" Stewart yelled and put the cup in the holder beside him. When he looked back through the window, a man was pointing a pistol at him, inches from his brain.

"Get out," the man demanded. "Now."

Stewart calmly and slowly opened the door, and the stranger backed away. Stewart stood between the door and man.

"Your money," the man said. "All of it."

"Okay, fine," Stewart said with his hands up. "You win. You can have what I got. Just don't hurt me."

"I hope I won't have to. Just give me your money and you'll live to see another day."

"I hate to inform you that I only have change in my pocket. Dimes and nickels from the vending machine. My wallet is in the back seat in my bag. Should I get it for you?"

"No. I will. Don't need you trying anything funny. What pocket of your bag is it in?"

"The one right there on the front. The only one. You'll find my wallet there. It's the only thing in it."

"Open the back door if it's locked. Slowly do it. No quick movements."

Stewart cautiously reached down the side of the

driver's-side door, finding the unlock button. He hit it two times to be sure. "Go right ahead."

The stranger kept his gun on him, and with his other hand, he swung the back door open.

Stewart watched, waiting for the perfect time to retaliate.

As soon as the stranger's eyes left Stewart and focused on the bag, Stewart kicked the back door. It slammed against the man's body. The man slouched in pain for a moment. But a moment was all Stewart needed. Again, he kicked the door, dropping the man further. And with a final kick, the door slammed against the side of the man's head. The gun fell to the ground. A second later, the man folded into Stewart's back seat.

Stewart grabbed the gun from the ground and aimed it at the person in the back. It appeared he was still breathing but far from consciousness. A small trail of blood was coming from his temple. Stewart looked around. There was a lonesome van parked beside him. He knew it was not there before. Perhaps this man had followed him off the highway. It was the only car around.

But it was not the only voice.

From the van, Stewart heard crying. Inside, an infant laid in a car seat. Searching the rest of the vehicle, he found a roll of duct tape and a large emergency blanket. He took all of it, including the child. He put the baby in the back seat of the car beside its presumptive father, the rest of the things in the front with him. Less than a minute later, everyone was gone. Only a van remained in the parking lot, unlocked and abandoned.

A mile up the road, police found a professionally-made mask of a man, a wallet with the identity of Stewart Hess in it, and a license plate, assumed to be taken off alongside the road and replaced with another.

After investigation, Stewart Hess had gone missing in Montana back in 1999. His body was never found; he was now presumed to be one of Valurie's many victims, nearly confirmed by the photograph found online, one with a shovel and bow, taken somewhere—who knew where—in Montana during the same year.

8.

THE FOLLOWING MORNING, the world could not believe what they were seeing. Valurie Bide's website was active and so were her social media accounts—and it was not winter! She had posted only a single photograph. It was simply titled "Colorado. 2020." And the caption of the picture on all formats read: "Happy Hunting. Glad to be Back. Better Hurry."

It appeared the photograph had been taken in the early-morning light somewhere, its precise location in Colorado a secret. The sky was a blend of oranges and reds as the sun rose. A mountain peak stood in the right corner, nearly black. The only real light in the picture came from several rays creeping over a lower section of the mountain range, creating a small glow on the ground. And in that patch of light was a shovel with a red bow attached at the top. Beside the shovel, almost radiating in the rays of light, was a child resting in the grass. It was wrapped in a silver blanket, alone, waiting for rescue—one that would need to be quicker than hungry animals and the coming rain.

"PLETHORA BEYOND THE GATES"

1.

THE FAMILY MADE a half-moon shape around the bed in the room. There was a constant hypnotic beating, chirping the heartbeat that still remained in Milo Hooper.

Milo was eighty-eight and lying heavily where everyone believed would be his last place of rest before retiring to the ground. Through Milo's eyes, he knew there were people in the room with him, however, they were vague, blurry, cigar-shaped entities. And they all seemed to be crying, saying his name at select times. The longer he focused on the noises in the room, the people standing around him, the more nothing made sense, as if that concentration, that energy, was being irresponsibly used to figure out where he was, who was with him, only to lead him to more confusion. The noises grew smaller, almost distant, and his vision…his vision effortlessly went to darkness after the thin slits that still gave him sight pinned shut.

There was a moment of peace for Milo, followed by the digital sound of his heart stopping….

One collective yell then echoed the room.

Hopefully these were not the last things he had heard, the final details comprehendible in his quickly fading mind.

2.

WITHOUT ANY RELATIVE recollection, Milo found himself in the middle of a field, beautiful and flourished with thick green at his feet. He noticed that his lungs were moving in ways they had not for years. The air here was…too pure; he could breathe almost too well, better than ever before. In realizing this, memories started to come back to him.

Yes, he had been growing sick for weeks and eventually hospitalized. So why was he here now in this place? He felt a heavy sorrow just then, figuring there could really be one explanation for his sudden recovery, his odd teleportation to his field. He was dead, but he was not alone.

In the center of the field was a towering hill. People marched towards it, some trekking near the top. The more he stared at it (How long did he stare? Was time relative here?) the more be believed he recognized this location. Or…at least this was something similar to a favorable spot from his youth, a place he loved coming to as a child during the winter. His neighboring friends would collect their sleds and spend the entire day climbing that hill and coming back down at a much faster rate, with much wider smiles and senses of excitement. But there was no snow here, nor his friends, not this time, only those people in the distance climbing the hill without their sleds and winter apparel, only wearing white shirts and slacks, exactly like he was. What he did find odd, though, was no one was behind him, no one spontaneously showing up as he had. If he were dead and this place was where you went after your immediate demise, would there not be people continuously finding this spot?

People die all day, every day. There had to be an explanation, perhaps closer to the length of people. Maybe they were after the same answer. And so, Milo took his first steps in this new place, finding that his legs never felt so strong, his heart working without hesitation or fatigue, his vision crystal, his hearing sharp.

To his surprise and disgust, the higher he climbed this hill, the air diminished in quality. It was much harder to breathe, and his nose kept catching a terrible smell as the light wind circulated this aroma closer to the hill's peak. Despite this field being lush with green, there was no scent of grass here, only...garbage? Yes, there was a sour, ripe smell here, coming from a place he could not see. But he had to press on, had to see where the people ahead of him were going. They were all out of sight now, all crested beyond. He turned around for a brief moment, and still, he was the last in line. Maybe this was not the afterlife after all. If not, then where was he?

At the top of the hill, Milo noticed the landscape had flattened, creating a smooth walkway. And in the distance, he could see only two people. One was walking to a set of iron gates, and the other was positioned by the gates, waiting. Milo guessed he was a guard or gatekeeper of some kind—perhaps the keeper to the afterlife, he was the one who let you in through the gates to what awaited everyone. And there it was: Milo was dead and ready to prosper into the next life. It all waited for him beyond the gates, even the smell.

To Milo's alarm, after the man ahead of him went through the gates, the keeper then began to close them. Milo ran, but that did not stop the keeper from locking the gates.

There was an audible, metallic bang, and the gatekeeper turned around. He saw Milo coming and knew there was a conversation to be had, one neither had ever expected to hear.

The man at the gate had long brown hair and was wearing the same white shirt and slacks like Milo, like everyone. He put up his hands and peacefully (his voice was terribly soft) asked Milo to slow his strides, that there was no reason to run. Milo heard him and gradually went back to walking, making his way to the one waiting for him, questioning what exactly was going on. Why was he being stopped? Why was there still no one behind him? Milo stopped just feet from the man at the gate. He looked past the man for a moment, for he was amazed by the gates. He had always heard about the gates that led to the afterlife but never truly believed he would see them, regardless if he knew death was inevitable. He had thought that maybe of all things that could be fabricated about life after death, he wondered if there really were gates that led the way. And, well...here he was. Milo looked down, back to eyelevel with the keeper. There was a hurt in the keeper's eyes; Milo could see a wetness, and something deeper behind, something...troubling, it seemed. Regardless, the keeper put on a simple smile and finally spoke again.

"Milo," the gatekeeper said. "I would like to welcome you to the afterlife."

Milo's instincts were correct: he had died, and this was the afterlife. He remained silent, knowing that there was no question now. He would never see his family again. At least, not for a while.

"My name is Michael," the man at the gates said.

"And do not worry about your family, you will see them again quite soon."

Milo looked at the man dumbly, wondering how he knew he was thinking such things. "Are you some kind of...angel?" Milo asked.

Michael looked at him and nodded. "Yes, something like an angel. I am the one who sees over the ones making their transition to what awaits them."

"Then why have you shut the gates on me? I know you didn't for the others. I saw the one before me pass. And if this truly is the afterlife, why am I the only one here now?"

Michael shut his eyes.

"What?" Milo asked. "What's wrong? Why are you stopping me?"

Michael opened his eyes. Milo noticed they were wetter than before. "I have stopped you because we are full."

"You're full? Full of what?"

"People," Michael answered. "We are full of people. And there is no more room for anyone."

Milo's mouth hung open. "How is that—"

"Possible?" Michael finished. "How is that possible, you ask? Honestly, it is quite easy to explain."

Milo looked at him, waiting, almost furious despite the cloud of heavy confusion. "Well..." Milo continued.

Michael let out a sigh before getting to his lesson. "Milo, as you now know—and can clearly see—the afterlife is real. It is where all the dead have come. Every deceased person for thousands and thousands of years has climbed the very hill you just have. Every deceased person, good or evil, for thousands and thousands of years has walked through those gates, their souls cleansed and forgiven, claiming their own piece of land. But what you and every-one else may not understand is this: The afterlife is not endless space. It is a dimension just like yours on Earth, a place and time that feels just as real as the life you know. Only, time does not stop here. Time does not exist here. So every person that walked through those gates is *still* here, alive. The ones that died long before Christ walked the Earth, yes, they are still here. Now, try and imagine what I have just told you. Every person who has died before you is in this location. Think of the world on a giant scale, but only a giant scale. Not infinite land. Can you even begin to im-agine how many people there are here? Think of the biggest city in your world, and just copy and paste them, right be-side one another over and over again. Can you even begin to understand how loud it is here? Endless voices that never stop. Can you imagine how terrible the true smell is beyond the gates? I know you can smell it, but think about what it really must be like? It is the scent of countless people, stacked right next to one another, in never-ending time."

Milo said nothing as his mind straightened all this information out, which was a chore. He was not sure if he could comprehend all the people over thousands of years that now live here. Every single one! The constant conver-sation would be maddening, be believed, yet it was impossible to guess as to how loud and annoying hearing that many people would be. And God, the smell. The smell that would never end, like a full-to-the-brim garbage can. And that imagery made more sense than anything. That is what the afterlife had become: a full trashcan, plus the constant chatter. People and homes stacked on top of one another, making room for the next, in a landscape with limited space. Would it really be worth it to live like this? To beg Michael to allow one more to live forever in this…chaos.

"If you ask me," Michael began, "it is not worth begging me for entry. It is out of my hands."

Milo started to cry. He had heard such things that awaited him in the afterlife. And yes, those things were perhaps still waiting beyond the gates, but there was no room for him. There were only…questions now.

"So now what? What's going to happen to me if I can't enter the afterlife?"

"You have been given a great chance, Milo," Michael said. "You will be given the chance to be with your family again. I told you that you would see them again soon. Did I not?"

Milo nodded.

"As you appeared here, you will appear again where you were just before finding yourself in our field. I cannot guarantee you how much time you will have once you return, nor can I tell you what to do with your remaining time. But I would cherish your family more than you ever could imagine. Make memories, tell them you love them. Tell them whatever you want about this place. And that will be your decision. Do you tell them the truth, or do you not put such imagery and hopelessness into their minds?"

"What will then happen when I truthfully die?" Milo wondered. "Where did all the people go that normally would've followed me up this hill? Where are the deceased going?"

"To occupy the rest of your rightful land," Michael said. "You have more than we do, and in more aspects than just land. You have space and time. We do not. We have endless voices and noise, you will not. You will have no reason to smell what we have once you are committed to the silence of the earth. So make your memories, enjoy your senses now. And enjoy the silence and cleanliness that awaits, for I will never know such a place and time. Good-bye, Milo. Best wishes on your return. I wish you all the happiness and joy with your remaining time."

Milo looked back at Michael with sorrow. He was in awe that even an angel could be so unhappy in the place we all wished to go. "I hope that you find some sort of peace here again, too, Michael."

3.

"DAD! DAD!" MILO'S son yelled after hearing the heart monitor next to him come back to life for no reason at all, signaling that Milo's heart was beating again. The rest of the family stood close by, in amazement, in…fear. "Dad!"

Milo's eyes batted. And for the first time in days, his vision was clear, almost as if he had brought back a few senses with him from the afterlife. Yes, he could see his son and two daughters, and all their children. God, they looked beautiful in his eyes, despite the tears now clouding his vision. Everyone else in the room was crying, too. Milo's son came in close to his father, touching his hand, noticing a warmth that was missing not long ago.

"Dad. You were declared dead. You were gone for

minutes."

I was dead? So why am I here now? Milo thought He said nothing, could only think, trying to find memories.

"Where were you, Dad? Where did you go?"

Everyone watched and waited.

"Mi—Michael. Michael," Milo said.

Everyone looked at one another, shaking their heads.

"No, Dad. There's no Michael here. We don't know any Michaels."

"Yes, Michael. The keeper."

Everyone remained confused. Everyone except for Milo.

His memories were coming back quickly. He had met Michael at the afterlife gates. He was denied. There was no more land to be given to the dead. There was only time on Earth now, no afterlife waiting for us. As he sat there, digesting this all over again, he knew he had quite the decision to make. Michael said he would be put in this position. What was Milo to tell his family? To tell them the truth about the afterlife, perhaps thereafter damaging all belief and hope for people? If anything, Milo supposed, people believing in the afterlife was a reason to carry out being a good person, for the duties of a good person will surely land them a spot in the next life. Milo knew he had tried to be a decent man his entire life, hoping that in doing so would provide him with existence after death. But no, that was not right. Every person, with their soul clean and exonerated, made it to the afterlife. But now the afterlife was full. Or was the best option to let it be, to enjoy the time he was gifted, to make memories again, let people continue thinking that there must be something waiting for them instead of the silence in the depths of the earth? Something good. Milo felt like he had such power with this knowledge, but…was it worth it? To let the world run amok and in fear, knowing their good deeds would never be worth the effort again if there was not a promise for life after death? Would anyone even believe him, for that matter? This was a responsibility that seemed bigger than he, bigger than human minds, bigger than…our world. And perhaps that is all that was needed to know: that we should continue knowing little that is not attached to our planet and dimension. Let people keep believing in something better than what they may have right now. But Milo knew this life was all he would ever have, all anyone would forever have from this point on.

"Dad," the son repeated. "Who's Michael?"

Milo looked at his son and then to everyone in the room. "No worries. He was only a person I met once. His memory had just come back to me."

"Did you meet him in the place you went after death?"

Milo debated his decision, the outcome it would have on his family, on the world, if the truth spread.

"No, son. I met Michael, what feels like a lifetime ago, at an old sledding hill, a place I used to go to every winter as a child. Memories I didn't know I still had but must still cherish." He looked at his family, his eyes wet, though feeling better than he last knew. "It's perhaps a miracle from God to see you all how I see you now. Come on, let's find out how to get me out of here as soon as possible. I don't want to be here. The smell of this place is horrible."

"CRAWLING RAIN"

WHEN MY EYES opened—blinking rapidly, trying to remove the remaining sleep from my eyes—I found myself in the living room of my home, resting heavily on the couch. Normally, I would've lain there after a mid-afternoon nap, trying to remember the dream I had, searching for the motivation to get up and away from my position. However, there was an awful distraction stopping me from piercing back into my subconscious any further, not allowing me to move. It was a familiar noise, I believed. The rain?

Indeed, I heard the falling rain and storm come in, that faint, dinging dance in the distance, then transition into the beautiful music of hypnotizing tapping on the roof above me. The more I listened, though, the more I began to question this sound's nature, power, its substance. This— whatever was touching down on my roof—was harder than rain; it was solid, echoing the environment, nearly rattling my home in constant vibration the longer it continued, which was ever-going, no sign of stopping anytime soon. The noise grew remarkably as I waited, listening. It was much more dominant than a typical—even torrential— downpour. Something seemed wrong; ever since the launch of this…this…nightmarish uncertainty, something was entirely off. There was the chance, though, that the rain was simply coming down *that* hard and steadily.

But really?

My gut turned, almost if I knew better.

I had never feared a flood in this area—my location too high, the air too dry—but I knew this was unusual in some way, for my heart was starting to race organically at the questionability above. It was fear I was feeling. Nothing but fear.

And yet, it was my vision—not my gut or heart, but my eyes—that I thought had failed me after opening the door, seeing my back yard....

Quickly, I pinned my eyes shut in disbelief, certainly anxiety. I left myself in this self-inflicted darkness, hoping that when I came back to the light of day, the shock in my body would leave and the movement in my yard would stop, disappear entirely, prove itself to be solely a product of my imagination, my head still dreaming.

But I'm only a wisher, a dreamer, simply and flatly. Because when I opened my eyes, my property was still crawling with a variety of insects, all alive, all recognizably active and moving, creating a hallucinogenic surface on the ground.

They continued to fall from the sky as far as I could see, reverberating through the entire neighborhood.

Then came the panicked voices nearby....

"THE RISK OF WORSHIP"

1.

WHEN DENNIS KRANE looked through the airplane's side window, he guessed it would be another thirty feet or so until he would be back on the ground; hopefully, that is. He concentrated on controlling his breathing at that moment, trying to lower his heart rate back to a somewhat normal pace, but that was only so good when facing the unknown in an unfamiliar territory. Paranoia began to set in, naturally, but he needed to be rescued. That was number one, ideally the focus. He needed to be saved.

He released himself from the pilot's seat, feeling his head, noticing some tacky blood smeared above his brows. Dennis winced, detecting the trauma went deeper than skin. A possible contusion? Concussion? The plane barely had enough room for himself, and in the slight void he did not occupy was his—what he called— "survival bag." It was a small black backpack which contained the bare minimum he believed would be needed if a tragic event ever occurred and he survived to tell the tale.

And there he was, alive....

Dennis slowly reached for the bag, not attempting any sudden moments in chance the plane would suddenly shift while being suspended in the towering trees. There were several species of fruits hanging nearby—pineapples and oranges at first glance, perhaps others in the distance. The plane had not moved in the slightest after the bag was in his hand. Quite a good sign. Dennis centered himself back in the seat, opening the small pocket on the front first. He retrieved his phone, activating it.

Please let me have a signal, he thought.

And according to the icon in the corner of his phone, there was not.

"Shit." He figured he needed to get out of this dense forest and closer to open water, where he hopefully could contact someone, especially since he had not logged his flight (or any of them in the past) with air traffic control due to flying in a location categorized as Class E airspace. Dennis waited, gathering courage, and slowly opened the door beside him.

Again, the plane did not budge, suggesting it was *really* lodged and stuck in not one but several trees of absolute strength, stature, and age. With his bag in hand, he eased out the side and wrapped his arms around the thickest limb he could reach. His feet found a similar branch below. He stood there, looking down, strategically seeing his way before any more movement towards the floor of this alien place. But before he moved at all, he looked to his side at his plane, knowing she would be missed and wondering what exactly happened to cause this, something other than a freak accident.

Perhaps that is all it ever was since there was no other rational explanation for the sudden crash.

2.

IT WAS SUNDAY, which meant after church, Dennis, a bored, single, forty-six-year-old pilot got his never-used survival bag and hopped into the small, private aircraft he had purchased years before. He owned many acres of property along the coast of Texas, south of Houston; there was plenty of room to have a small hangar built to shelter his plane, let alone a proper runway and landing strip, all of which had been done professionally and with precise attention.

After takeoff, it was not long before there was a sense of complete openness as he flew over the gulf. It was just…him…and this hypnotic energy the absence of atmosphere created. When the weather was perfect—the sky clear of clouds, the same hue as the water below—it seemed there was nothing but Dennis floating alone in a void that never ended, no horizon line, no separation of sky and sea. Only space and time, and yet neither really seemed to exist during those moments of memorizing freedom.

An act of letting go and no one to see.

He had a traditional, repetitive route over the water, in areas that were deemed safe to fly over. He knew when he had hit his halfway mark—his turn-around point—when he would see a familiar landmark: a small island in the middle of the gulf.

It was roughly three miles across and the same in width, producing thick, vibrant trees of presumably many species. (And certainly he was proven correct after landing in the middle of the forest, witnessing the produce emitted by the healthy greens.) There were no buildings; it was an innocent island, untouched by human hands and their modern minds, still native and pure.

Dennis had done research about the island but found little online relating to it, perhaps due to the fact that it was…normal, even predictable, since it was not odd to see others exactly like it (or close to it) scattered and dotted throughout the water on his customary Sunday trip.

Dennis looked at the fuel gauge and then again through the window, telling himself he should be seeing the island any…

And there it was in the far distance. A mere speck of green in the ocean, that small interruption in Dennis's complete nothingness that made him become fully aware again.

"Time to turn around. Almost halfway already," he said, feeling thirsty, considering his bag where he knew some water bottles were. "The flight's going quick to—"

His tongue froze (did he bite it?), and his eyes grew wide when a cloud of thick smoke started pouring from the engine, only feet from where he sat, blurring his vision almost entirely through the windshield. His eyes went down slightly, looking at the dash. Every gauge was failing, each pinned to a position as if they were off; all electronics that lit up the interior were also dead, blank, staring back at him like a black mirror, assuring him this was a serious problem—*the* problem most every person in flight has feared but never had to experience, face. An internal battle started, one that contradicted the rhythm of his heart, one of fear and the opposing instinct to stay calm, get this plane and himself on the ground. But the only land visible in the never-ending blue was the small island, his recognized landmark. He knew this was not going to be easy, and did not know whether he would make it out alive. A staggered beating continued in his chest.

The plane continued to dive, losing altitude as Dennis kept himself in line with the island. He was only several feet above the tree line when he first passed over the shoreline of the island. The trees were so green from this lowered vantage point. His face was covered in sweat, his hands shaking, questioning his strength and mental stability to keep the aircraft in line. There were loud scrapings on the undercarriage of the plane for just a moment before the nose of the plane went under the tops of the trees. A chaotic harmony of broken wood and bending metal followed. Dennis closed his eyes, prayed, and nervously waited for the final impact, unknown where it would be. Perhaps Heaven.

The plane was thrown around by the collisions as it ripped through the landscape, cutting it like a knife. Dennis jolted side-to-side in his seat. And a moment later, all had quieted after a harsh stopping; not a landing, but an instant halt. Dennis's heart was pounding when he returned to the back of his seat and opened his eyes. He had survived. By God, he had made it, categorized as a rarity. But he knew he was not in the clear. He was stuck; his plane was suspended in the air, balanced and buoyed by nearby trees of support, holding him and his dear life.

3.

WHEN DENNIS FELT that familiar feeling of the ground under him, he opened his bag and retrieved his phone again. Still no service. Scoffing, he put the phone in his pocket and looked above to the plane and trees. He was in complete shade, like being trapped in a bubble. The air, though humid, was exceptionally clear, fresh, free of pollution, buzzing with a variety of insects. At his feet, he noticed the floor of the forest was littered with fragments of splintered wood and debris. In the distance, he could see that part of the left wing of the plane was not too far away. He stood there a moment, collecting his breath, convincing himself that he was, in fact, alive and okay. Thankfully only a headache and cut above the eyebrow. Rescue was still needed, and so he had to start moving to where he could locate a cellular signal, which he believed would be closer to open water, away from the blocking shade of the rich and tall canopy. If he could *not* get reception there, he could at least create a fire signal to address urgent help in the vast openness of the shoreline, a clearing where he would not damage the nearby forest with an uncontrolled flame.

Dennis determined he was roughly in the center of the island. Any direction he chose to go would bring him to a shoreline in the same amount of time, give or take. He pulled a pistol from his bag, tucked it into his waistline, and slowly started to walk, following the stripe above him that his plane cut through the forest. And it was not long before he knew he was not entirely alone.

Dennis could not be entirely sure, due to the thickness of vegetation and, perhaps, the ache in his head, but he kept believing he saw movement, followed by sharp noise, as if something were running close to his location. This happened several times within the first ten minutes of exploration, causing an unclassified type of anxiety. He was alone, wandering in a place he did not know or understand with a feeling of being hunted, even spied upon. Thankfully, that sensation started to evaporate when another ten minutes passed without any signs of life, that worry slipping away. Or was it getting worse? That knowledge of absolute isolation sinking in, that absence of help. He could not focus on that; he had to keep moving.

Stay positive.

He had already made it thus far.

The rarity. Continue to be that.

He came to the peak of a small incline and supported himself against a tree. The heat and humidity were draining his body, his ambition. Dennis opened his bag and got a bottle of water, chugging the majority of it. He told himself to rest a moment, sit and recharge in the shade. Peering down into the small grove below, he could not believe what he was seeing.

Were they...tents? Here?

If they were, they were like no tents he had ever seen, perhaps too far away to define exactly. This uncertainty did, though, assure him there could be people here— or were here and had left. Maybe biologists? Maybe help!

Slowly, Dennis made his way down the embankment and towards the tents in the distance. The forest here was less dense; there were indications of trees being removed entirely or chopped down, leaving only stumps and stray shreds of bark. There was no sawdust, though, eliminating the consideration of a chainsaw in the proximity. Through the remaining forest, the tents were growing; he was getting closer, noticing that there was a small circle of space cleared of most vegetation, though the towering trees nearby continued to hide their location, that spread of thick green and shade, for he had never noticed such a spot when flying over this island many times before. At the edge of the clearing, Dennis emerged and digested exactly what he had stepped into finding.

First, he counted—one, two, three, four…twenty-two; twenty-two large tents were erect in this spot, varying in size, though all miniscule compared to the smallest home he had ever seen. They were made of stray pieces of wood (perhaps from the trees that were uprooted from this opening or in the nearby forest where it was less dense). All were wrapped and woven with green. Broad and long leaves and plants had been intelligently weaved through the wood like a basket. On the ground, several feet from him, there were…axes? Dennis squinted at them, telling himself that if he were to see these specimens elsewhere, he would have guessed they would have come from an early stage of civilization, maybe even showcased in a museum, documented as history. They were awfully simple yet obviously effective (due to the creation of the tents) and plenty used. There was a sharpened rock at the end of a thick stick, wrapped again with green—some kind of strong and durable plant. There were a couple that had a red rock, but after kneeling to them, Dennis assumed that the discoloration on the stone was blood. Animals' blood? Had to be, he predicted, even though he had not seen any animals (but there was the movement in the forest), because not too far away, there were large leaves on the ground, one with small piles of raw, darkening meat. The more he looked at it, acknowledging and accepting, the more he noticed his other senses were picking up on the rotting smell and sound of the flies on or around the stacks of muscle and fat. There were loads of feathers and bones next to the meat. *Bird meat,* Dennis thought. The other leaves held fruits and nuts. A stack of sticks was to Dennis's right, assumed to be yet-to-be-made arrows since many laid beside the sticks with a spear-like stone or tapered bone attached at the end, wrapped in green. Smaller baskets were scattered throughout the property, some containing what looked to be hardening clay, others wet on the bottom, like they had been dipped in water—or at one time held water. Maybe from the fish that were resting on the ground nearby? Or was there a freshwater source near this location? How or where? Did they use ocean water and somehow clear, filter the salt? *If* they were drinking ocean water. What else were they drinking, though? They needed some type of hydration. What Dennis did not see, oddly, was a fire—or a site where a fire had or would be built. This puzzled him. He guessed that due to the location, there really was not a need to stay warm; the yearly climate would be survivable without it, he assumed.

But what about the meat on the ground? How did…whoever…cook it? Or did they *not* cook it? Raw consumption?

Dennis continued to observe, but only for a moment. There was noise—loud, stomping echoes—in the forest. And not just in one location but encircling him. Animals? Surely not birds. No….

He slowly spun in a circle, feeling a sense of being an animal in a cage.

Was *he* the animal now? Being hunted?

A spear landed beside his foot.

Dennis fell in surprise and…God knew it was fear.

Ahead of him, at the point where the forest started to grow thick again, emerged twenty—maybe twenty-five—people with spears in their hands. They ranged in age and height. Their bodies were almost entirely covered in a tacky gray (perhaps mud, clay?), smeared with other various colors. Dennis guessed handmade paint from other organic sources, like berries and mushrooms. Maybe blood. Each had long hair with feathers stuck throughout and wore a skirt-like dressing of long leaves, hiding their sex. To his left and right, another party emerged, chalked up exactly the same, just as many, but here, some were obviously women and young children. They all were armed, even the short offspring; if they were strong enough to hold a spear, they were.

He knew he needed to exercise caution and establish trust with this group, but his mind was sprinting with questions—ones that he guessed would be left unanswered.

Where did they come from? Were they always here? If so, how long is "always?" Were they perhaps owned by other people at one time, only to be dropped off here to figure out survival? Or were they left here to be forgotten?

A past unknown.

Dennis turned back to the initial group. "I'm trying to get to the coastline," he yelled.

A mixture of grunts and noises came from the ones before him. A language unfamiliar, maybe even old, forgotten.

"I was only passing through," Dennis continued. "I wrecked my plane that way." He turned around quickly, scaring the ones behind him.

They drew back their arrows as if they were ready and willing to release. And then he saw the others to the sides do the same. Dennis heard movement coming behind

47

him. He needed to halt the threat. He reached into his waist-line and a second later pointed his pistol in the air. He fired. Every arrow in sight fell to the ground; all hands went to their ears. It appeared they had never heard such a sound, such power. They all looked at one another. Dennis turned back to the ones who were approaching. They looked just as confused.

"I'm no threat. Only trying to get myself help. Go-ing to the coast," Dennis said, putting his gun back in his waistband. He used his hands to gesture the act of walking and pointed in the direction he wished to continue.

They stood looking at him, questioning.

Dennis tried to move forward.

The ones before him quickly reached down for their arrows.

"No. NO!" Dennis yelled, putting his hands up, waving them, distracting the ones before him.

How can I get out of here? he wondered. *I can't shoot my way out of here. If they've never heard a gunshot before, maybe I could show them other things they haven't seen.*

Dennis slowly reached behind him, removing the backpack from his shoulder. He knelt to the ground and opened it. Sweating, he pulled everything out and displayed what he had to the onlookers: two rolls of toilet paper (one for its general purpose and the other to help start a fire), a baggie of lint, three lighters, two bottles of water (one mostly empty), several pop-top cans of beans, fruit, and tuna, a hunting knife, a small stack of rags, and several squares of rubber to create black smoke for rescue, if ever needed.

He opened a can of beans, brought it close to his face, and smelled the contents. Dennis looked up to the ones before him, signaling them to come closer.

They did not move, a trust yet to be created.

A trust needed to be established that had yet to be done.

So Dennis dipped his fingers into the syrup and beans and ate what he had hooked. He could see the onlookers' stance change from stern and cautious to a sense of relaxation and wonder. Dennis predicted they had never seen food in a can, let alone an aluminum can at all, the near effortless action to feed hunger in a modern world. But this world was not modern.

He again motioned for them to come closer. Only one did, presumed to be the alpha ahead of him. He had the most red smeared on his face. As the man came closer, Dennis again had another quick helping of beans, trying to convey the safety of his offerings. The person came closer until only the items from the bag separated him from Dennis. Dennis handed the can to the man. Taking it, the man held it in his hand, feeling the weight, recognizing the sugary smell inside as it passed under his blue-tipped nose. The two looked at one another, and then Dennis motioned him to sit with him, to share and learn. And to Dennis's disbelief, he did.

They sat across from one another. Dennis watched and waited as the person put his fingertips into the can, then to his mouth. The whites of his eyes grew in amazement, probably feeling the inside of his mouth doing—reacting— in ways it never had before. A flood of salivation, intensity. Dennis smiled at the man, nodding. The man returned the gesture, but he seemed curious about the other foreign materials before him. Dennis felt a nervousness start to run through him. He knew there was not enough canned food to feed them all, yet he believed there was something he could show them that would be of benefit to everyone, forever.

Reaching, Dennis grabbed the three lighters from the ground, putting one in each hand, the other in his pocket. The alpha, with smeared bean sauce circling his mouth, looked on; everyone by the edge of the forest watched, too. And with a snap of his thumbs, Dennis ignited the lighters, letting the flames dance right above his hands. The man ahead of him went from his knees to bowing.

Is he kissing the ground? Dennis questioned to himself.

It was then that everyone also bowed.

Dennis looked around. *They have never seen fire,* he thought. If anything, he guessed, they had only seen it organically coming from the heavens, perhaps striking down on the forest causing authoritative damage. *That's why there's not a firepit anywhere.*

The alpha slowly looked up. He had tears in his eyes.

Dennis released the lighters, and the flames went out.

A frown of disappointment instantly grew on the man's face instead.

So Dennis flicked the lighters again, effortlessly creating fire.

The alpha again bowed and started a sort of chant near the ground. Echoes around him started, surrounding Dennis. The more these noises continued, the more Dennis believed they were singing. And it was undyingly beautiful. Some were humming; others had a high-pitched song. Were they singing about the fire? Rejoicing over what Dennis brought to them? Worshipping him? Was he the Almighty one now? Would the newly inherited title allow him to move onward to the coast?

Christ, what else would be needed, to be seen as more than a god?

He chanced standing and no one moved. He took a few steps, and no one moved. Dennis motioned to a pile of rocks nearby, gesturing to bring some to his location. The alpha, still on the ground mesmerized, made a grunting noise to the ones closest to the rocks. Each of them carried as many as they could towards Dennis. They laid them at his feet. Dennis took each and placed them beside one another until creating a small circle. The onlookers were confused. Dennis again pointed, but this time towards the sticks, hoping he could collect a few without the crowd thinking he was stealing their future weaponry. The alpha voiced the same tone, and the sticks were delivered to Dennis. He sat around the ring of stones, snapping the sticks into smaller pieces. The alpha especially looked worried, upset, maybe seeing a day's work being broken right in front of him. Regardless, he only watched. They all did.

Dennis stacked several of the sticks in the center of the stones, creating a triangular shape. He turned around and went back to the display of items, grabbing a roll of toilet paper and the lint. Unwinding the paper, Dennis removed a long ribbon of white, ripping and rolling it into individual balls, placing them inside the sticks. He then put a chunk of lint in the center. Instead of going back for the lighters, he pointed and motioned (flipping his thumb) to the alpha if *he* would be the one to bring the devices over. The alpha snatched them up and went to Dennis's side. Together, they knelt by the wood and stones. The alpha tried to give Dennis the lighters, but Dennis only took the one. He flicked down and the fire came. He again motioned his free thumb, trying to teach the man how he could use it himself. It took several attempts, but when the alpha had fire above his hands, he and everyone cheered. Dennis smiled and released his lighter, letting the fire go out. The alpha did the same. The flame went out. Again, Dennis ignited the lighter. And just the same, so did the alpha. The singing started again. Dennis took his lighter and put it near one of the balled-up pieces of toilet paper. It went up in a smoldering flame. He gestured to the man to do the same, to learn. The alpha reached in close, feeling the warm by his hand and his arm, and a moment later he had succeeded.

Dennis and the alpha backed away, watching, smiling. Dennis then went to the sticks, grabbing several and placed them on the fire in the stones, showing them that more wood would create a bigger fire, one that would be longer-lasting. Pointing to both the meat and fish, Dennis motioned for them to be brought to his location.

The alpha huffed.

Dennis put his hands up. "No. No. This will help you," he said.

There was silence for a moment. Perhaps the food was solely theirs; maybe they were unwilling to share or use that for demonstrations, for unworldly magic tricks from the gods. The two stared at one another until the alpha finally gave the go-ahead gesture, but signaled something with is hands, like cutting the air slowly. Only one from the tribe moved, and he only brought one piece of fish and two small portions of bird. After bowing—thanking—Dennis took a stick, piercing a chunk of bird muscle. He could feel all eyes on him as he put the meat over the fire. A sizzling instantly filled the stone, resonating a tone to everyone around. Dennis rotated the stick, cooking all sides of the flesh until figuring it was done. Anything would be closer to "done" in comparison to ingesting pounds of raw meat—especially bird—he presumed. Dennis pulled the muscle off the stick and handed it to the alpha, motioning to put it in his mouth.

And he did. His eyes widened. His mouth watered. His life changed in that instant.

Dennis was truly then a god to them.

4.

WITHIN SEVERAL MINUTES, most everyone that had been surrounding Dennis a moment before, guarding the line the dense forest, was cooking around the fire, learning, roasting both meat and fish—even nuts and drying fruit—cheering and bringing praise to Dennis. While they ate, Dennis showed the alpha how to make his own fire, and how to tie pieces of rags onto sticks to create a torch so he could transport fire with him anywhere he wanted and create it wherever needed. Soon, there were five fires all around the cleared-out area. People were dancing, enjoying this gift and this new way to eat their food. Some saw how to make their own torch and frolicked and ran around as if this were the best day of their lives. And perhaps it was. This brought Dennis a great sense of helpfulness and purpose, but it was help for himself that he still needed. He had to get to the shore. Dennis returned to his belongings on the ground. He bent down and unrolled a bunch of toilet paper, then took the lint and rubber squares, putting everything in his pocket, feeling two lighters. The alpha still had the other.

Dennis reunited with the alpha, walking him over to the items from his bag still on the ground. He pointed to everything and then to the alpha, gesturing that he could have everything that laid before him. Dennis reached in his pocket and handed the man one of his lighters.

"Keep it. Keep everything," Dennis said.

The alpha looked at him. More tears rolled down his face. He might not have been able to understand the words spoken to him, but at the same time, he did. The alpha was being gifted these material things, along with the new education of fire.

Dennis knew deep in his heart, though, that the lighters would only last so long. And he wondered if that was perhaps the best in the long run: they would eventually be returning to their normalcy. But for now, let them enjoy the modern.

When Dennis recognized the bright acceptance in the alpha's eyes, he again pointed towards the forest, motioned with his fingers that he wanted to walk out, hoping to get the alpha's assent. The alpha pointed in the same direction and softly nodded. The gifts and offerings had worked; they had been accepted. Dennis returned the nod, and a minute later, the crowd, fires, knowledge, and his possessions were behind him as he ran past the last small tent and into the thick green ahead of him.

5.

IT WAS THE sound of a bell that stopped Dennis's racing.

A bell? Why a bell? Why here? Where would it be coming from? Then it hit him….

He slid to a stop and wildly reached into his pocket and looked at his cellphone. There was a single bar of signal—an icon of hope! The bell was a text notification, apparently, according to the timestamp, sent hours ago by his closest neighbor. *He can wait,* Dennis thought. *I can't.* Dennis called 9-1-1, giving the operator a detailed report of the crash, hiding the secret of the people in the forest. He waited while his call was being geolocated.

"I'm going to continue to the far-western side of this island. There's a shoreline I can get to for rescue. Please send help there."

Dennis placed the phone back in his pocket and started to cry.

He was going to get out of here after all.

It was not long after Dennis fell to his knees in the sand on the shoreline before he heard a wafting noise coming close, followed by the silhouette of a helicopter in the distance. He got to his feet and ran to the edge of the water, waving his hands, jumping up and down. The helicopter hovered near while a ladder was deployed from the carrier. Dennis practically jumped into it and crawled up until being greeted by rescue. Safe at last.

As the helicopter took off with everyone aboard, there was a heavy mixture of concern from everyone when the pilot coursed over the island looking for the plane. But it was not the plane they first saw. No. What they saw instead was a huge cloud of smoke and a blazing fire towards the center of the forest.

Dennis's heart dropped. As did his mouth.

"Jesus and Mary," one of the rescue personnel yelled to anyone listening, then looked over to Dennis. "Did you see the fire when you were in the forest? How could such a thing happen? Was your plane the cause of it?"

Dennis shook his head, thinking. "No," he said. He was certain it was not because of his plane.

Maybe someone took a lit torch into the trees, running, cheering, playing—handling something they did not fully understand and the forest ignited? Maybe they took a torch into their home and it had caught ablaze? Maybe they had been still singing, rejoicing Dennis after his departure, only to have their songs of joy abruptly turn to screams as their homes and land burnt, as they watched each other burn alive. If so, they were probably still burning now as he effortlessly flew over them, safe, alive, thankfully unharmed.

Dennis was glad to be saved, yes, but at what cost? He looked out the window and started to weep, his body filling with a sense of guilt. He knew he was responsible for the fire; he had given the crowd something they were not used to, and they had not known how to properly care for it, correctly respect and secure its power, unknowing to how out of control it could quickly get in the wrong hands and excited minds, then spreading violently in a vulnerable environment. The creation of fire was to be a gift, not the origin of a possible genocide, the annihilation of an island. And yet it burned...becoming smaller in more ways than one, Dennis knew, as the helicopter furthered itself away.

"UPROOTING"

WITH OUR SHORT time here on this planet—the days and years somehow seeming to get shorter with each rotation around the sun, our provider—it's quite rare to hear a discovery that changes history, a ripple of new information that fills in old gaps in the timeline or contradicts it. What's even rarer is knowing someone that has been involved with such an upending of our understanding of the world. I know I was there, sitting there with my brother and our father when we found it, our eyes and brains not quite able to work properly, unable to fully comprehend what was before us since the plausibility of the discovery was almost laughable, only found in the most abstract of dreams. No one found anything too funny, though. We were not dreaming; we all knew we were awake. And at one time...*they* were, too....

It was near the end of March, the temperature finally comfortable enough to be outside for a longer period of time, the majority of the day, and the ground completely defrosted, the creatures in and above the earth starting to roam again. The year before, my brother, Mickey, our father, and I finally came together and purchased nearly twenty acres on the crest of a ridge in Northern Pennsylvania, a nearly two-hour drive from where we lived and grew up together. The land had belonged to a friend of my father. He had inherited it and never used it, and needed to sell it to settle a nasty divorce. When I was growing up, I remember Dad always saying he wanted to purchase some land one day, build a nice camp for all of us to come to for whatever reason: hunting seasons, a weekend getaway, a place to escape our future wives. "You'll understand one day, boys," Dad had said to us when we were still living with him, long before leaving for college. And there was absolutely nothing wrong with our mother; my parents had a healthy relationship and still do, but I must admit, I did later in life understand how a few days away could cool off some fights, make you see things more clearly when you returned and apologized.

We were eager to go back once the winter had passed, visualizing what the land one day would be. Our vision had grown—influenced mainly by the whiskey at Christmastime in our father's basement—into the idea of a small family compound with a cabin for each of us. That way, if we needed (in the rare event) to get away from each other, we could. Plus, we could personalize our own living spaces. We were separate people after all.

We knew there were years of work ahead of us since all of us were still working full-time, knowing we would only be finding time to get up there on the weekends during the non-snowing months. After purchasing the land, there was a lot of paperwork before we could even remove a single branch from the property, writing checks, and getting the ground prepared: having each property mapped out by a professional surveyor, having them document everything for the courthouse. Then more crews for the drilling for the wells and multiple septic locations, making sure electric could be run in the area. This year, what needed to be done first was cutting the remaining trees down in each of the properties, then having an excavator create several pathways from the road so a crew could come in and dump the concrete foundations. It would take a lot of work and money to remove it all, but the vision of our small empire was what we always came back to, smiling. We planned, though, to utilize as much of the trees as possible, using the wood for our cabins, making our floors and walls. And when possible, keeping as many standing as we could. There were several down on my brother's property alone that we had no desire to try and cut down without help. They were the biggest trees we had ever seen, especially in that area. Several of them had a terrible bend and appeared ready to snap or fall in upon themselves at any moment or...any year. We had the capability to cut down many of the trees ourselves but, holy hell, we would, without a doubt, need professionals or the help of Mother Nature for the ones that looked almost alien to the area. And it was only the Mother that had shown up during the winter....

My father parked the truck at the edge of our property, what one day would be the beginning of the driveway that led to his cabin. It was just above forty degrees. We were dressed in jackets and gloves. We each carried a chainsaw and pistol, just in case. As we walked into the forest, we had no idea what to expect. It had been a hell of a winter—record snowfall, high winds, days without power in certain areas—and within several minutes of walking, we had spotted a handful of fallen trees. My father made a joke that it would be less work for us to cut down. Laughing in agreement, we kept moving.

At the very peak of the property, we sat and had lunch, dividing up a couple sandwiches and beer. Here was where my father and brother's property connected. After finishing my portion of the sandwich, I pardoned myself to smoke a cigarette away from them since they were still eating. After a few minutes of mindlessly walking, just exploring and looking around, enjoying the quiet, I found a nice rock to sit on. I removed a cigarette from the pack and reached for my lighter. But I stopped, noticing that one of the huge trees on my brother's property had fallen...taking out many in its path, creating this long cavity in the woods.

"Yo! You guys better come see this," I called. "Looks like a massive hole in the ground down there when it came up from the earth," I said to myself and finally ignited the end of my cigarette, placing the lighter back in my pocket. There were quick footsteps coming closer to me.

"What is it?" my brother asked.

I pointed.

Dad came up beside us, groaning. "Now that's a mess," Dad said.

And he was not wrong.

Just from where we stood, we could see a massive oval shape of opened earth, like someone had opened a large soup can, leaving the lid up. There was an impressive system of roots (the root wad) attached to the bottom of the tree leading back down into the ground, resembling thick veins of some kind that were still connected to the organs inside a body. The length of the tree laid to the right of the roots, creating a massive void in the woods, a long strip of leveled trees, the result of massive weight coming down on them, bringing them to the forest floor.

"Let's head down there and get a closer look," my brother recommended.

With curious, wonderous ambition, we went to the

site.

It was our eyes that were the most perplexed once we stopped and investigated the hole the tree had created, the opening below the root wad. I know I rubbed my eyes, blinked rapidly to make sure my focus was correct. My brother did not say a word, and my father, all he could mutter was: "Dear God."

Inside the hole, there was a hauntingly human-like skull the size of a bathtub. It had much more of a cone-tipped crown than a human skull, and there were roots from the tree weaving and navigating through the eye sockets, which were nearly as wide as my own body. Some of the teeth were still attached, resembling sharpened index cards. Others lay on the ground beside the skull.

"It's a grave," I remember saying. "A grave for a giant."

"How is—"

"I don't know," I said, interrupting my brother.

"I need to sit down," my father admitted.

Below the jaw of this skeleton, I could see more bones, perhaps the start of a spine. But most of it was lost or hidden beneath the earth where the hole ended, transitioning back to level ground. There was more to it. Maybe an entire skeleton. I paused that thought, though, and turned, looking throughout the forest. In this spot alone, there were three other trees of this size. My mind started to accept what I didn't entirely want to.

Yes, there was more to this.

Throughout that spring, we had more people on our property than we honestly wanted: researchers, scientists, historians, excavators, loggers. The estimated age for the tree that had uprooted was nearly seven hundred years old. The same went for the others of similar size. Upon a scan of the earth around these other large trees, a startling discovery had been made: there were more skeletons at the base of these trees. This was what I had initially wondered or...feared. These trees were not just trees, but gravestones, markers of some kind, planted purposely, precisely above the head of an ancient, unknown skeleton. Perhaps this was ritualistic after another died, a remembrance of a humanoid being that walked this land long before any of us. Since our discovery, thirty-four other superior trees have been reported within a few miles of our property and they all are scheduled for subsurface scans. I can only assume what lies under them, or...what could still be hiding below our feet.

After their removal from the ground, each of the four skeletons on our property were just shy of forty feet in length, their weight assumed to be well over a thousand pounds. Aside from the exaggerated bones and proportions in anatomy, there was one detail that stunned everyone. These creatures possessed a tail. Each skeleton had numerous bones hanging off the back of the spine. Were they for balance? Fighting? These questions started countless theories for many interested parties.

It's not so much that I fear what we've found; I have no reason to fear what no longer exists. The problem is I'm now entirely curious to what else, near or far, could be lost, the remnants of ancient time, what happened here before us—before humans first wrote themselves into the timeline of the world.

"THE BALANCE"

1.

PHILLIP DEADMAN FINISHED making love to his wife. He softly collapsed next to her ear and told her that he loved her—a gesture he always made, even expected on the receiving end.

"I love you, too," Tori said.

He smiled against the darkness in the room and carefully moved off her, sitting on the edge of the mattress for a moment, catching his breath, regaining feeling in his legs before chancing to move.

"Going for your smoke?" Tori questioned, though she knew the answer coming.

Phillip turned to her. "As always," he said, for he always had a cigarette after sex. He nearly had a pack a day, but he routinely had one after certain exercises: eating, sleeping, sexual endeavors. "Need anything while I'm down there?" he asked as he stood and went for the dresser, getting a pair of sweats and a long-sleeved shirt.

"Just for you to come back."

He smirked. "I always do. Looks like it's still snowing," he said, pointing to the window where strands of sparkling white tumbled softly and innocently.

"So pretty," Tori whispered, closing her eyes, satisfied and tired.

Phillip made his way to the downstairs kitchen where his cigarettes lay on the table. The small electric candles in the window frames throughout the home guided him with minimal light. The shadow of a Christmas tree stood strongly in one corner of the living room, taller than him, and much more beautiful than himself, he believed, when lighted up. Wrapped boxes stayed hidden in the thicker blackness below the tree, as if clandestinely watching him pass by.

Beside his cigarettes was an unopened bottle of whiskey—a gift he had received earlier that night from his Secret Santa, Kenny Loudens, senior accountant, at the annual office Christmas party. Phillip and Tori were nearly drunk when they came home from the social gathering, neglecting the whiskey altogether to instead indulge one another. But now that the sex was over…hell, why not? Phillip removed the plastic sealing on the lid, tossing it into the sink on his way to get a rocks glass. He poured himself an overflowing shot, recapping the bottle. He sniffed the glass. "Ah," he voiced. "Beautiful." He took a sip, letting it sit in his mouth, that relationship being made. "Damn good," he said after swallowing. "Damn good, Kenny." Phillip went back to the table and claimed his cigarettes, then put on his boots and coat by the back door.

Phillip sat his whiskey on the porch railing, chilling it slightly in the couple inches of snow as he lit a cigarette. He grabbed the glass again, watching the snow, feeling a familiarity that he did not care for. "It was a night just like this," he said, turning toward his neighbor's house to the right. He could only see the top half of the home; a tall wooden fence bordering Phillip's property blocked out the bottom portion, stopping at the edge of the house. A row of short shrubs created the line for the rest of the property, separating his front yard from the Cobb residence. He stared at the dark upper windows as he sipped and smoked. "About two years ago now," he said to himself. "Poor girl went through a lot, and I hope she never has to deal with such a—"

A light suddenly came on in an upper window of the Cobb house, interrupting Phillip's thoughts. Phillip waited, staring, smoke rolling from his nostrils. A startling scream came from that exact direction, followed by a series of high-pitched cries from the same voice. He stared in alarm, listening.

The lights in the room began to flicker rapidly, as if someone were flipping the switch as quickly as they could. The screaming continued.

Yes, it's a female. Macy, Phillip thought. *But is there another voice, too? I think I can hear someone else.*

The windows then exploded. Phillip jumped back in shock, slipping in the snow. The whiskey glass fell from his hand, staining his snowy-white surroundings; the cigarette smashed into the porch boards when Phillip caught himself from the fall. Several pieces of glass from the neighboring window landed in his yard—and other nearby locations later found. Another scream caused Phillip to look up. Smoke was now rolling out of the upper windows, and there was a warm glow flickering behind the thick of gray.

"Dear God, the house is on fire—and Macy's inside! Oh, no! God no!"

Phillip threw himself back in the house, racing to the phone on the wall, skidding to a slippery stop on the tile floor. He dialed (more like punched) 9-1-1, just as he did nearly two years for an accident at the same house. A dreadful feeling of déjà vu hugged him closely, but it did not cause him to feel any warmer. Panting into the phone, Phillip gave the responder a witness account of what had happened, plus an address.

"Police and fire departments in your area have been contacted and are en route immediately. Stay where you are, sir. Do not go onto the property. Do not put yourself at risk as well."

Phillip slammed the phone down. The lights behind him in the living room kicked on. Tori stood there, squinting.

"Are you okay?" she asked, eyes still adjusting.

"The Cobb's house is on fire," Phillip replied.

Tori's eyes instantly went wide, instantly awake. "Oh, my God! Is Macy home?!"

Phillip nodded quickly. "I heard her screaming."

Panic claimed Tori's face. "Okay, calm down." She hummed a moment. "The screaming could be a good thing, right? She's alive, awake! She isn't sleeping through this. Probably just screaming 'cause she saw smoke and fire. I would, too! We should stand outside and wait for her to come out," she finished and opened the closet, retrieving her coat.

"You're right. Let's go."

They ran out the front door, leaving it hang open. Flashing lights and sirens were in the not-so-far distance. "Jesus," Phillip said, stopping in the yard, looking back and above him to the Cobb home. The entire top of the house was engulfed in violent, lapping waves of fire. Witnessing it, Tori began to cry.

"Come on, Macy. Get out of there," she said.

Phillip grabbed his wife's hand and together they raced to the edge of the shrubbery, sliding as they rounded it. Other neighbors ran toward them, some already standing on the sidewalk at the edge of the yard under the streetlight.

Phillip and Tori stared at the door, waiting. They could see light in the bottom windows of the house.

But they could also see fire....

"Come on, Macy. Come on, Macy. Come on, Macy. Come on, Macy," Tori huffed. "Get out of there."

The police and firetruck were in sight, cresting the hill—that damned hill from two years ago.

Someone down the sidewalk yelled: "Do ya know if the girl's home?"

It sounded like Matthew Davis.

Phillip looked that way. "Yeah she—"

The front door of the Cobb house burst open and Macy appeared, sprinting until falling face-first into the snow. Fire rushed through the door as if it were chasing her, wanting her back inside.

Phillip ran to her, taking off his jacket on the way.

Most others watched, frozen in amazement.

Macy began screaming and tried to get up, but Phillip threw his arms and coat around her.

"Stay still, Macy. It's Phillip. You're okay; you're out. Stay still. Breathe. Quiet. Tell me what happened."

But she only continued to scream....

The police cruiser and firetruck entered the property just as Tori was wrapping her arms around Macy, trying to calm her down, examining her. Some of Macy's hair was burnt, much shorter, along with several bruises and cuts on her face.

The policeman rushed over to the three while fire-fighters raced through the yard with hoses.

"Get an ambulance over here," the policeman said over his radio.

"NO!" Macy screamed, scaring Phillip and Tori back into the policeman. They all fell to the ground and listened as Macy continued her screaming as she stared at the house.

"No! Let it burn! Let it burn! You must let it burn!" Macy got to her feet and ran towards the closest firefighter that held a hose. "LET...IT...BURN!" But she did not make it any further. She dropped to her knees, defeated. "LET... IT...BURN!"

2.

"OFFICER," A NURSE began after sticking her head out of the doorway, "it's okay for you to see her now."

The officer stood from the bench in the hallway and entered the room, passing the nurse. He was eager to talk to Macy that morning, for it was nearly impossible the night before as she was hysterical. Once the ambulance came, they took her straight to the hospital for tests and examination. Thankfully, her smoke intake was not entirely severe, the cuts on her face minor, and the bruises on her body would heal, doctors assured. Her hair would also grow back.

"I won't be far," the nurse began. "Ring for me if you need anything."

"Thank you, ma'am," the officer said, nodding, as

she left the room.

Macy Cobb rested on a hospital bed, eyes wide, looking out the window, not acknowledging the policeman in the room.

He went to her bedside.

"Macy," he began, "my name is Officer Risper. Shawn Risper. How are you feeling this morning?"

Macy slowly looked over to the officer. He was shorter than she expected; his voice suggested a much larger, thicker man. She predicted he was only a few years older than her, perhaps pushing forty. "Did it burn to the ground?" she asked.

The officer sighed. "I'm sorry to say that it did. For the most part."

"That's the best thing that could've happened."

The officer squinted at her, confused and curious. "Well," he started, "that's why I'm here. I need to know why you thought it was best for it to burn. You kept repeating that last night as well. Do you remember?"

"I remember everything," Macy hissed, frowning at him.

"Good," he said. "Because I need you to run me through what happened. How did the fire start? Did you start it? You obviously thought it was best for it to burn than to be saved."

"No. I didn't start it."

Officer Risper studied her eyes, what *they* were telling him. He hummed a moment. "Then who?"

"I was attacked."

And by the ungodly fear he saw in both her eyes and face and the small snarl in her answer, he knew she was telling the truth.

"So you weren't alone? Someone was there with you? Who attacked you, Macy? I'm going to need you to tell me everything. Can you do that for me?"

She sighed and slowly nodded. "I can, but," she paused, thinking, "the story goes back to when I was just a young girl, when I was seven, I think. When my father and I moved into that house after my mother passed."

"I'm sorry to hear about your mother. Truly." The officer grabbed a chair and sat beside her. He removed a set of keys from his pocket and put them on the stand next to her, then grabbed his notebook, unfolding it. "Ready when you are. Start from the beginning."

"Okay," Macy started, "but it wasn't a person who was in the house with me last night. Not exactly."

3.

IT WAS OCTOBER 10th, 1990, and it had been raining all day, heavier at times than others. The temperature of the day had also been a near-record low. Macy and her father were sitting around a shyly furnished living room, still scattered with more boxes than places to sit. There was at least a couch, and their beds were assembled upstairs so they had a place to properly sleep. They had only been moved into the house for two days. But it was their own, even if developing its personality was a slow process. A fireplace burned slowly; sparks popped and flared periodically from the drying wood. For now, a single photograph of William, his now-deceased wife, and Macy rested safely above the flames on the center of the stone mantel. Overtop the smell of burning logs, a miasma of boxed macaroni and cheese hung through the house. William was resting in his recliner, his eyes focused on a small floor-model television that sat in one corner, streaming what little the antenna in the window could pick up. The volume was low but loud enough to block out most of the reverberating sound of rain outside. Macy played aimlessly with her dolls and plastic horses, spinning in circles. There was a tremendous crash of thunder, scaring both of them. Macy ran to her father for comfort, shaking on the short way there, kicking some of her toys to the side. A moment later, the power went out and it rained harder than ever. William held his daughter.

There was another crash of thunder, shaking the house.

"Shh—" William voiced, calming his daughter's cries. His hand combed through her red hair.

After what felt like an eternity for Macy, the lights decided to come back on, illuminating the living space. The sound of rain persisted, but no longer did it echo like automatic gunfire on the metal roof. The sight of her toys was enough to get Macy off her father's lap. William walked to the kitchen where he reset the time on the microwave after looking at his watch: 8:40 p.m. He peered out the kitchen window and merely saw the silhouettes of dead tree limbs, only visible due to the few streetlights at the intersection of the road.

There was a light knocking on the front door.

Macy called for her father.

William looked foggily in that direction and started toward the door. Macy let go of the horse in her hand and began to prop herself up. The horse balanced on its thin legs before toppling over to one side, still smiling—for a plastic horse is always smiling, showing its endless, human-made expression of joy. William reached for the doorknob as Macy stood close beside him, as curious as her father.

Once the door was sufficiently ajar, both father and daughter looked dumbly into the night. A face dimly glowed from the porch, the borders of the corresponding body lost against its black clothing and the dark of the night. William reached for the light switch next to the doorframe. A screaming bright light above the person at the door revealed (what William and Macy figured was) a man wearing a jet-black trench coat. The hardened, spiked shadow of an umbrella covered most of his face. There was a suitcase in one of his gloved hands. The man at the door tilted his head and locked eyes with William. The man's eyes looked dark, nearly hidden in the shadows. The stranger studied him a moment, focusing.

"Yes?" William questioned, breaking the silence.

"Good evening. I apologize it being somewhat late," the figure at the door said. His voice sounded brittle, old, but harmless.

Cautiously, William put his arm across his daughter's torso, shielding her, then eased her to the backside of him.

"Please," the man said, "there's no need for that. I mean no harm. Honest. I'm on my way to visit an old comrade of mine. I have another day's drive ahead of me yet before we are reunited. It has been many years since I've seen him, sadly. So when I knew I was going to be passing close to here, I made sure to put it on my list to stop on this very doorstep. I'm staying at the hotel up the way. So I don't have further to go, nor was this stop out of my way. You see, I'm here because I'm a friend of the prior owners. I used to stay in this house and sleep in one of the upstairs rooms when I'd travel through each year while I was in the circus."

William chuckled. "No kidding?"

"No kidding, sir. Last time I was here was, oh…" The man stopped to think. "Maybe fifteen years ago. Let's see, I'm seventy-five now, and I retired from the circus at age sixty. So yeah, fifteen years. I know I'm standing here now, but it's hard to believe that I'm here again." The man shyly smiled. The light above him danced off the curved edges of his teeth. "I know this must seem out of the ordinary, especially at this hour, but, my heavens, it's been a long time since I've stood foot at this home. Would it be possible to take a look around? Just for the sake of nostalgia? I'll be on my very way then, I assure you."

"Daddy," Macy said, "he's getting more wet. And colder."

The man at the door chuckled and weakly knelt to Macy's height. "My...you're a sweet girl, aren't you?"

"My dad says so all the time," Macy remarked.

"I'm sure he does."

"Macy, please..." William started.

"Sir," the man at the door said, "I assure you once more I'm no man of harm. Here, let me give you this. I have definitive proof my word's true." The man put his suitcase down near his feet and reached into his pocket. William stepped further in front of his daughter in anticipation to what the stranger may extract from his pocket. Could it be a knife? A gun? There was no way to tell, but William could not take the chance. The stranger took out his wallet, giving

William an old black and white picture. "Take a look. That's me standing in front of this house back in 1935. And here," he said, handing out another photograph, "that one was taken in the same spot ten years later. That's my wife there beside me. Sadly, she died shortly after that photograph was taken. Last picture we took actually. Terrible accident in Wisconsin while the circus was there. She was incredibly balanced, like a tightrope goddess, except for that day. She fell more than sixty feet." The man wiped at his eyes. "Never gets easier, ya know? Even after all this time. And now, no one wants to spend their time with a wrinkled pile of bones." The man tried to laugh.

William sympathized with the man, knowing exactly how he felt. And perhaps that alone made his guard go down significantly.

"Come on in," William said to the stranger, giving him back his pictures. "Macy, be nice to this man. Don't bug him."

The man smirked. "No worries at all. I thank you for allowing me in. I assure you."

"Excuse all of...this," William said, pointing around the room. "We haven't been living in the home very long. Still putting a lot of stuff away."

"Oh, my. I feel even worse to be imposing on you then."

"It's not a problem," William admitted. "I hope this brings back some memories for you. Can I get you something to drink before we take a walkthrough? Brandy okay?"

"That does sound delightful on a night like tonight."

"Macy, be a good girl and take the man's coat. We

can put it on the back of one of the chairs in the kitchen."

Macy reached her arms out towards the man. First, he put his suitcase down beside him. Beads of water rolled down the luggage, settling on the tiled floor like a tiny pond. He folded up his umbrella and handed it to her. Macy stared at his shining, bald head. Slowly, he removed his gloves and placed them in Macy's hands. The man's hands appeared dry and cracked despite the constant hydration of the rain outside and the sweatiness of his palms. There were small, lavender spots on the back sides of his hands, probably due to age. He slid off his coat and folded it into a sloppy square, giving it to Macy. Under the jacket, the man wore an aged sports coat and slacks.

"Wow, that's heavy!" Macy cried once she had the coat balanced in her arms.

"Try wearing it, sweetheart," the man answered, smirking.

"Please," William started, "take my seat." He pointed to his recliner. "I'll be right back with the brandy. Come on, Mace."

"I apologize in advance if I dampen your chair."

"No need to explain," William assured the man. "It's just an old, ratty thing anyway."

"Thank you," the stranger said and sat, inspecting the house.

William and Macy returned a moment later.

"Here you are, sir," William said, handing the man a small glass of liquor. "Ready for the tour?"

Macy frowned. "But...but Daddy, I didn't even show him my horses or dolls."

William snorted a small laugh. "I'm sure he doesn't

care to see—"

"Nonsense!" the man interrupted. "What are their names?"

"You can tell him their names and then it's off to bed, missy," William said.

Macy practically ran to the circle of toys spread out nearby. She picked up her dolls first and recited their names to the man: Amy, Heidi, and Elsa. She put the dolls down near the man's feet and came back with the plastic horses, introducing them to the man as well. "Beauty, Pickles, and Kiwi. Kiwi's my favorite," Macy admitted. "She has the best smile. See?"

The man pulled the cup away from his lips. He reached for the horse. "Ah, yes. A pretty smile, indeed. But they all have pretty smiles, don't they? Even the dolls."

Macy grinned, taking the horse back and starting to gallop it around on the floor and up the chair around the man's face, voicing a continuous "click-clock, click-clock," trying to impersonate the sound of heavy horse hooves.

William perceived this was annoying: a small child bouncing a plastic horse around an old man. This was not why he was in the home. Though, the man wore a smile, still.

"Macy," William began, "you better get into bed. I've already let you stay up much later than normal."

Macy's frown extended further than before. She held Kiwi in her hand, holding it by the leg. "Come on. We can show the man the upstairs first. How 'bout that?"

"Okay," William agreed.

Macy reached out her free hand to the stranger, as to guide him out of the living room and up the stairs.

William and the stranger got up from their spots, smiling.

They marched up the stairs to the landing where a small hallway connected to several doorways. One was the bathroom; the others were William's bedroom and a room chaotically filled with office equipment. The hallway curled to the left and led to another door, that being Macy's room. Macy let go of the stranger's hand and ran down the hall, rounded the corner, and stopped by her door.

"Come see my room," she cheered.

"It isn't much to see right now," William confessed. "Just her bed, dresser, and boxes, I promise."

The man chuckled and went to Macy. He stood in the doorway, looking around the room, bobbing his head softly.

"Bringing back any memories?" William wondered, approaching them.

The man looked back at him. "Oh, yes. Many. This was my bedroom. Every year."

"You used to sleep in here in my room?" Macy asked.

"Uh-huh," the man started, "for many, many years. It's a good room." He looked down at Macy and smiled.

"Okay, Macy. Into bed," William said.

Macy stuck out her bottom lip.

"Pardon me for just a moment," William began. "I'm gonna tuck her in and I'll be right back out. Feel free to look around up here."

"No problem, sir."

"Tell the man good night, sweetie."

Macy looked at the man a final time. "Good night."

She yawned immediately after.

"See, you are tired," William said, walking his daughter into the room. "I'll be right back."

"Take your time," the stranger insisted and walked back towards the other doorways, turning on their lights, looking around, not seeing what he was looking for. Yet, he had already knew it was gone the moment he walked into the house.

It was missing from his vision, and the black had returned.

4.

"SORRY 'BOUT THAT," William said as he exited Macy's room.

"Please, no apology needed. You have a wonderful, sweet daughter."

"Thank you. Find anything in either of the other rooms?"

"'Find?' No, sir. As you said, there isn't much to see, let alone find."

They both laughed a moment.

"But there sure are the memories. Good memories. Good friends. God, where has the time gone?"

"Tell me about it," William furthered. "I can't believe Macy's seven now. I hope she continues to do as well as she has since the passing of her mother not quite a year and a half ago. I can't believe it's been nearly that long as well. Damn."

Sorrow filled the man's face, suffocating his wrinkles. "My condolences, sir. I noticed the picture above the fireplace. Beautiful woman."

"I thank you for that. Cancer took her." William paused, considering how to continue the conversation without crying. "Another brandy before you leave?"

"I'd accept. Yes. Thank you."

William motioned for the man to lead the way down the stairs.

Macy heard their departure. She opened her door as quietly as she could and stepped out. She looked out over the railing and sat, listening to what her father said: "You can follow me into the kitchen if you want. Table and chairs in there where we can sit."

"Very well," the stranger said.

Macy then moved to the stairs and went down like a mouse.

The man sat on the chair holding his coat, looking around the room.

William placed another shot of brandy in front of the man and sat across the table from him.

Macy proceeded into the living room, hiding behind the wall, eavesdropping, learning about the past.

"So you said you used to stay here every year? And you became friends with the prior owners of this home? What did you do in the circus?" William trailed off. "Forgive me; I apologize. I think all this moving has my head a little tired. I don't think we have even introduced ourselves yet. My name is William Cobb."

The stranger reached out his hand. "Gunnar Westfield."

They shook.

"Uh, yes. Way back in thirty-five. That was my first

stay here. And lucky for the Masters family, I did come into this home. They needed me. Did you have the pleasure of meeting them? We stayed close over the years, so I know they had moved out and had an estate agency sell the home."

William glanced at the man. "No. I never did meet the prior owners. I only dealt with the real estate agent. But I'm confused. Why was it lucky that you stayed here with them? What happened? I'm intrigued. Please, continue."

"Very well."

5.

GUNNAR WESTFIELD, AGE twenty then, stepped off the train and made his way to the information stand, confirming his next departure. Everything was still on schedule, noting that his train to New York was still on for six-thirty the following morning. He had an afternoon and evening to kill, and more importantly food and shelter to acquire before then.

It was a beautiful late May afternoon in the small town of Lewisville when he stepped out of the station. He was at the edge of a parking lot where several cars sat, some empty, others inhabiting one or more people, presumably waiting for one of the passengers filtering around Gunnar. He noticed there was a road to his left leading to…he had not the slightest clue. And to his right, another road led to a two-lane bridge. Distantly he could see houses in that direction, sunken in deep from his higher location.

A well-suited man was walking towards Gunnar.

"Excuse me," Gunnar said to the random male passing by him, going towards the entrance of the station.

The man spun around.

"Are you from here?" Gunnar asked, putting down his belongings. "This town."

"Yes, sir. I am. Leaving shortly, but yes. How can I help you?"

"Unlike you, I'm not from this area. Nowhere close really. Chicago. Anyway, my train doesn't leave until tomorrow, and I'm in need of a place to stay and eat. Is there a hotel near?"

The man gestured toward the road to the left. "Don't bother heading that way. You're actually on the outskirts of town currently. The only things up here are the train station, the lumber yard, and the papermill." The man then pivoted and pointed to the bridge.

Gunnar turned.

"Now, if you were to head back that way and walk alongside the bridge there and go, oh…about a mile and half towards the center of town, you'll find a nice, little place to stay for the night. Just opened not too long ago. You'll find several places to dine on your way there—and after, too. If you can't find it or get lost, I'm sure someone will be outside and able to help you out along the way. You'll start to find homes and shops soon after crossing the bridge. See 'em down there?"

Gunnar nodded.

"But I think the hotel's on Atherton Avenue. Just stay east."

"I appreciate that. And as far as transporting myself to the hotel, can I get a cab or is walking my only option from here?"

The man shyly laughed. "We do have a tiny cab

company, solely created for people like you getting off the train. You could come back in the station with me and give them a call if you want. But why not embrace the day? The sun's shining, the birds singing. Plus, you're a young buck. You'll make it just fine. Get yourself a good look at our little town." He laughed again. "Anything else?"

"Not a thing," Gunnar responded, grinning. "And yes, I think I'll take a walk. Good idea. Been sittin' on that train for most of the morning. A little exercise and air would do me good, I imagine. Thanks for your help."

"Of course," the man said. "Welcome to Lewisville. Don't expect much though, you coming from a big city. We are small, but we are friendly. Have a good day." He turned and entered the station.

Gunnar smiled and nodded. "You, too," he softly replied, the man nowhere near him. He picked up his luggage and briefcase and headed toward the bridge and the town below.

The man Gunnar had interacted with was nothing but honest. As he walked on the side of the bridge, the cars that passed him were cautious, the passengers even waved as they went by. There were a variety of ages below him, fishing from the river under the bridge. Conversation and laughter rose to him. A smile came to Gunnar's face, unintentionally, but he noticed it. At the base of the bridge, he crossed the street and continued on a sidewalk, finding (and smelling) homes with freshly mowed yards. There were children playing on either side of the street, running, chasing. There were adults in the flower beds, weeding, cleaning, picking, and planting. Some were washing vehicles or their homes. The air was incredibly clear. There was hardly any traffic, even when coming down from the station. This place was pure, simple; unknown to Gunnar. There was a calming, fresh personality about this town already, Gunnar believed, a sense of pride in happiness and cleanliness. This, though, was an initial thought, the first minutes into the relationship. Maybe the town of Lewisville was not all like this; perhaps the center of town is a mess? He did not know—and he never found out, at least not then.

At a four-way intersection, he paused, reading the signs, deciding where to go since none of them were Atherton. He had to move on and assumed to continue straight since he was only told to just stay east.

"Need help, fella?" a male voice said distantly.

Gunnar looked up, searching.

"Over here," the voice continued.

There was a young man diagonal from Gunnar on the opposite side of the road. He was waving and smiling, wearing a plain white t-shirt and blue jeans. His dark hair was combed back, and his face was shaven. Simple. Clean. Happy. "Yeah, over here."

Gunnar raised a hand and started toward him.

"Are ya lost or somethin'?"

"Possibly," Gunnar chuckled, hopping up onto the curb.

The man came down from the small front yard and onto the sidewalk, sticking out his hand. Gunnar noticed at this distance he could not have been more than five, perhaps seven, years older than he.

"The name's Logan Masters."

They shook.

"Gunnar Westfield."

"Good to meet you, Gunnar. What are you looking for?"

Gunnar put down his belongings. "I was coming from the station. My next train doesn't leave until tomorrow morning. I talked to a man outside, and he said that there was a hotel nearby. On Atherton."

"He was correct. Maybe a half mile yet." Logan turned and pointed up to a hill. "Crest the hill and keep going. Atherton will be on your right after a while."

"Thank you."

"Not a problem. But," Logan began, "if you'd like to save some money and wouldn't mind shackin' up with a couple of newlyweds, you could stay here with me and my wife, Hillary. We have a spare room upstairs that we have no use for, and recently decided to rent it out to a person like you—someone coming off the train and staying for a short time."

"You don't say?"

There was a little sign in Logan's yard. He pointed to it. It read: Single Room for Rent.

"It isn't much," Logan said, "but you'd have a room to yourself. No pressure. Completely up to you."

Gunnar looked at the man, studying him. *Only son. Father served and died in the war. Mother raised him. Worked on farms. Marriage. Moved to this house. I see them outside this house, their belongings being unloaded into the yard. But why can't I see further than that? All I see now is darkness. A sheet of black. I can't see them inside the house.* Gunnar thought. *He, himself, seems okay. No bad past to worry about.*

"You're a good man," Gunnar said. "I think I'll

accept your offer. Save me some walking, too."

Logan chuckled.

"And newlyweds, huh? That's wonderful. Congratulations."

"I thank you for that. Here, let's go in so you can meet—"

But the front door came open, interrupting Logan.

"Speak of the devil."

Hillary started down the yard, smiling, barefoot.

"Beautiful woman," Gunnar admitted.

"I know it," Logan smirked. "I'm quite lucky."

"You are."

Hillary stopped before them. She was rather short and wearing a cream-colored dress with sunflowers printed in various locations. Long brown hair fell down her back. Gunnar assumed she was around the same age and then studied her, too.

Loving parents. Good upbringing. Cattle farm. Oh, no, a fire at the farm. A rebuild. Nurse. Marriage. Moving to this house. Unloading belongings into the yard here. Now just darkness, that same sheet of black. That's all I can see after their arrival. Why can't I see them inside the house? Her Spool ends here, too. Something's wrong. But not with her. They are kind people. I need to see the inside of the house.

"Hillary," Logan began, "this is Gunnar Westfield."

"Gunnar, nice to meet you."

"Likewise," he replied.

"Gunnar's going to be staying with us tonight."

"Oh, wonderful. We've been talking about how great of an idea it would be to rent the room out. Lucky us!

We were right."

"You'll be only staying tonight, correct?" Logan asked.

"Correct. Train in the morning."

"Shame it won't be longer," Hillary said. "But we'll make the most of it! Oh, I'm excited to have someone stay."

"Well, let's go inside then," Logan insisted. "Get your things in your room. Probably get supper started in an hour or so. What do you like, Gunnar?"

Gunnar laughed and picked up his bags. "Honestly, whatever you're having, I'll accept. Thank you. That's very kind."

The Masterses and Gunnar walked to the front door and went in. Gunnar stopped as soon as he passed through the doorway. He began to study the house.

House being built. Owner. A traveler of some kind? A male. He wasn't here often. Women coming in the house with him.

The bags then fell from Gunnar's Hands.

Hillary gasped when she heard the noise behind her. She turned.

Satanism. Worship. The basement. Sex—orgies. Drawings. Blood. A murder-suicide ritual. Blackness. That same blackness, nothing else. Why the blackness again? Why is it blocking the rest of the history of this place?

"Are you okay?" Logan asked.

The blackness Gunnar could see remained in his mind's eye, and that *never* happened. History always finishes, and the present always takes over eventually, creating our current reality. And that is how it was for Gunnar when he could see a person's or a building's or a landscape's history. He called these quick glimpses of the past a person's or an object's "Spool." All he had to do was study whatever or whomever and then a thread of visuals would dance in his mind, seeing events and history, catching the important things along the way—the bigger, more impactful experiences, what changed something or someone. Then his vision would clear, reconnecting with present time. But the blackness Gunnar found in the house's Spool was not leaving his mind, almost physically blurring out the Masterses completely as he stood there. He believed this blackness was the sole reason he could not see either of them inside the house while processing each of their Spools. The blackness attached to this home was blocking that part of the history here—them inside, making early memories, leaving their thumbprint—as if it were stronger, more dominating than any special moment this family could create. And if that were the case, that only meant one thing: Whatever that blackness was, it was still about somewhere in the house. Anxiety found Gunnar's stomach. *This never has happened,* he told himself. *What is that blackness in all the Spools? Why is it blocking anything else? Why is it here, and why doesn't it go away? I don't like this. Something's wrong. I should leave. Dammit. No. I can't. There's a family here. I should do what I can to help. Just in case. They may need it. Because I have no idea what that darkness is.*

"Gunnar, are you okay?" Logan repeated.

"Yeah. Yes, sorry," Gunnar replied, batting his eyes. His vision was back to only seeing them. He picked up his luggage. "Darn things just slipped out, I guess." He chuckled. "Quite the house you have here. Doesn't seem too old."

"Not at all," Logan said. "Was built only a few

years back."

"Uh-huh," Gunnar voiced and put his bags back down, knowing a long conversation was to be had.

"Are you sure everything's all right?" Hillary asked.

"I hope so," Gunnar admitted.

The Masterses looked at one another, confused.

"Pardon?" Logan said. "What's wrong?"

"I'm assuming you both are familiar with what happened in this house?"

Hillary's mouth fell open.

Logan looked at his wife and then back to Gunnar.

"Just who are you, Gunnar Westfield? How could you know something happened in this house if you aren't from this area? Why are you here?"

Gunnar sighed. "I'm on my way to New York. I was told I'd be given a job if I could meet a man up there."

"What type of job?" Logan said with what was close to aggression.

"Please, calm down. I'll explain. I'm going to be joining the circus. They're setting up a spot in New York currently. That's why I'm headed there."

"How does one get a job in the circus?" Hillary wondered. "Does it have to do with how you knew something happened in this house?"

Gunnar nodded. "Exactly. I have this…gift, or ability, I guess you could say. Growing up, I thought everyone had it, but I learned quick with kids calling me crazy that I wasn't quite normal. I never told my parents or grandparents of this ability. However, I did tell my brother, thinking he too had this ability since we were twins. But no, he didn't.

My brother was jealous initially, but eventually thought it was the best thing, and later in life would exploit me, mainly for money. Make a bet with someone that I could see their past and then we would split the coin. That's kind of how I got this job. The circus was in Chicago last week; that's where I'm from. My brother and I went. By the exit there was a large sign that said: Got a talent? Ask for Marv at the entrance. My brother immediately told me I should go ask for this Marv person. He said this could be my calling. I didn't know much about that, but we did make our way back to the entrance. I asked one of the clowns handing out tickets if there was a Marv around. One asked if I had a talent of some kind. 'You could say that,' I replied. The clown gave his tickets to the one beside him and told me to follow him. My brother and I trailed him to a tent just beyond the circus grounds. Two men were sitting in chairs. One was much shorter than the other, and he was smoking a cigarette. He tersely asked what we wanted. Smoke seemed to come out of all the holes in his head, even the ears. The clown next to me explained that I claimed to have a talent. The short man wondered at first if I was a group act since we were twins, but I told him otherwise—that only I was auditioning. The man waved the clown off and asked my brother and me to approach. The bigger man—and by bigger man I mean he was near seven foot and built like a house—got up and motioned for me to have a seat. He walked to the back of the tent and watched us, stared really. The short man said his name was Marv. We shook hands, and then he told me to get to work, to tell or show him what I could do. When I told him that I could see certain events from a person's past, he annoyingly explained that they already had a fortune teller. 'But I can't see the future. Only the past. There's a difference.' He squinted at me, inhaling his smoke. Yes, smoke then came out of his ears, but when the smoke exited his mouth, he told me to prove it. I studied his face. *Family was part of the circus, too. They were just as short. He was never schooled. Traveled with family. Took over business when they died. Setting up circuses across the country past few years.* When I told him this, he said I was rather vague. That I had to tell him something only he would know. I leaned in close and whispered to him the rest of what I saw but didn't want to say aloud at that time. 'I know—or can *see*—that you were attacked not too long ago. You were locking up for the night. It was just you and...' I trailed off and motioned to the monstrous man in the back of the tent. 'You and that guy. It was dark and someone rushed you. He stabbed you, and then...and then your partner back there damn near killed him. You...perhaps...have a scar from the accident under your right armpit. Yes?' My brother cursed in amazement. Marv smiled and nodded and told me I had something special, that I belong in the circus, and if I could meet him in New York the following week, he'd have a job waiting for me."

"And that's why you're here," Hillary said.

"Precisely."

Logan sighed loud. "Did you see our pasts? Do you see everyone's history?"

"I did," Gunnar replied. "I call someone's past their 'Spool.' And I don't do it with everyone. It's *so* exhausting having to evaluate everyone you come in contract with. So I mainly use my ability for safety. I didn't see any of your Spools until you invited me, a stranger, into your home. I had to be sure you had a clean past—and you both do, I'm happy to say."

"But the house," Logan began, "how could you know about what happened in the house. The house isn't a person."

"Buildings and places hold just as much history as living people, often more. But this house, this house is new. So there wasn't much to see. But what I did see, I don't care for. And frankly there's something I see that's blocking me from viewing the end of this home's Spool. That bothers me. Do you know exactly what happened here? And I mean *exactly*. My ability only gives me so much—flashes of events that have caused a dot in the history line to a place or person."

"Why don't you tell us what you see, Gunnar? And we can patch the rest for you," Hillary said.

"Okay," Gunnar began, looking at the wall, watching his vision change before him. "I see the house being built—that's always the first with a building because that's like the birth of the Spool. Then a man bought it. He wasn't here often. I see him coming and going, sometimes with women. Then it gets bad. I see devil worship, Satanism. I see the basement and people drawing on the floor. A ritual. I see death and a suicide. Then nothing else. Only this wall of blackness." Gunnar than looked at them, his vision back to reality.

"You do have a gift," Logan admitted. "All that did happen here I'm sorry to say. People called us crazy for buying this home. But we needed it, and could afford it, for that matter. We just have to move on and make this home our own. Change its history."

"I'm afraid there's no changing history. What has happened has happened. But yes, you can make this home your own and enjoy it for a long time. And I may be able to help you while I'm here."

"Go on," Hillary said.

"First, why don't you tell me what I'm missing. I'm trying to figure out why I'm seeing nothing after the suicide happened here. I don't see either of you inside this house, and with you moving in here, living in it, creating memories, I *should* be able to see that plainly, but I don't. Only this thick blackness that blurs out anything further."

"What blackness?" Logan asked. "You've said that twice now."

"Yes. Usually at the end of a Spool, the images in my mind disappear, like forgetting a dream almost. But this house's Spool doesn't do that. There's a blackness that remains. It blocks any images of you two in this house. And I don't know why. That's why I need your help to try and figure out what that blackness is."

"I don't know if what we know will help you," Hillary said.

"Please, try," Gunnar urged.

"Well," Hillary began, "when this house was being built, there was a rumor going around the area—we grew up here if you didn't know or *see* that already—that an outsider had already purchased the house. It was said he was a salesman of some kind, and our little town was right in the center of his travels. It was ideal for him, I guess. But you're right; he'd be gone for days at a time. And yes, sometimes he'd bring home several women at night. The neighbors said he was nothing but friendly when they would catch him outside on the rare occasion. Just had a thing for women, we all guessed. However, more and more gossip started when this group of young kids on bikes—they are still around if you'd want to speak with them—started to spy on what was happening in the house. These kids would hop the fence out back and look into the basement windows when word went around town that the salesman was back with more women. At first, the kids said that it was just one big orgy down there. They'd wear weird animal masks, apparently. The neighbors then began to say that less women were coming out than going in. No one really believed that though because who's to say when they left, either by car, bus, or train. And so, rumors began. We couldn't keep eyes on him all the time. But we should have. This went on for a while until the biker kids burst into the police station one night, claiming they saw a murder take place in the basement when they were spying on the salesman and one lone female. The salesman had apparently cut the woman's throat. Blood went everywhere, and the man started drawing and chanting. When the police showed up, they found him in the basement with his own throat cut. Your murder-suicide you saw. Upon further investigation, there were women's clothes scattered throughout the house, but no bodies or evidence that more deaths occurred here. More gossip spread in our area, though. We then bought the place after it was cleaned and sat for a while because no one would buy it."

"I don't believe any other deaths happened here; I don't see that, thankfully. And I'm sure I would if I can see the others. I wonder what the drawings and chanting was about?" Gunnar said.

"Maybe he was trying to summon something?"

Logan asked. "You did say 'devil worship' before."

"I certainly hope not," Gunnar admitted. "Tell me, how has the house been for you since you've been here. How long has it been?"

"Been here about six weeks," Logan said. "Honestly, the house has been nothing but great. We love it. We just have to sort of forget what happened here. I trust time will blur that out. Right, love?"

Hillary nodded. "It is a great little house for us."

"So nothing at all seems off?"

Hillary looked at Logan.

"What is it?" Gunnar continued.

"Well," Hillary began, "it's the basement. I know that it's been cleaned up, blessed, everything else to make me feel better, but, God, I don't know. When I'm down there to get canned goods, I often feel like I'm being watched. Just this feeling of eyes on me. Something waiting patiently. But I don't feel it anywhere else, really. Which I'm thankful for, and honestly, it's probably my mind making a bigger deal than it is due to me being in the basement, standing where such awfulness occurred. I agree with Logan and believe that time may blur out the unease."

"It could, I'm sure," Gunnar began. "But—"

"What is it?" Hillary interrupted.

"It's the blackness at the end of the house's Spool. It shouldn't be there. I'm going to tell you something, and I hope that you don't panic."

"Go ahead," Logan said.

"I think whatever that blackness is was created by the prior owner. Whatever he was doing in the basement could be the origin of it. In fact, I know it has something to do with it because the black doesn't show itself until then—nowhere during the salesman coming and going, not during the orgies. Not with the suicide, even. Whatever it is, came after he was dead."

"And you can still see it. What does that mean?" Logan said.

"I think it means it's still here. Creating its own history in this house, as if someone or something were—or is—living here with you, and you're all sharing this time, this moment, this...life together. Except all I see is *it*, that sheet of black. Neither of you. Nothing of you exists in this home's Spool. However, there's something I haven't told you. And again, I don't mean to panic you. But...I did see that same blackness at the end of each of your Spools. I saw it. So...you see...you and the house *are* sharing something together, right now. You're sharing whatever that darkness is. I'm telling you all of this because I feel I should... should...warn you. If nothing alarming has happened in the house yet, that's wonderful. I'd hate for that to change."

A row of tears rolled down Hillary's face. She was in fear. Logan put his arm around her, telling her that everything was going to be all right.

"Warn us of what? What would or...could happen?" Logan questioned.

"Logan, I don't know," Gunnar said. "That's in the future. I can't see that. And maybe nothing would ever happen. But I just...I just don't trust whatever that blackness is. It's strong enough to blur out the memories you and Hillary have already made in here. And I'm sure there are some aside from putting all your belongings in the yard."

Hillary then smirked. "The yard was a mess, wasn't

it?"

Logan laughed. "It was. And you saw that, Gunnar? Us in the yard with our things?"

Gunnar nodded.

"But nothing after that? For either of us?"

"Only the blackness you share with the house."

"Gunnar," Hillary began. "You had said before that you could help us, make this home our own. What did you mean?"

"I meant that I can give you something that will at least assure you there's a balance in your home."

"A 'balance'?" Logan questioned.

"Yes, a balance. I come from a very spiritual family. We learned to worship the land mainly. It was good to us— the land—but we also believed there was history in the roots, the bark of the trees we used for our home. And some history, especially things we don't know of, aren't always so pleasant. The world is full of both good and evil. There's that balance. We can't just have all good, and we can't just have all bad. There's a certain balance in the universe; there needs to be. However, it's undeniable that evil can visit at any time, especially if the forest has a terrible history. I say forest because we grew up in the mountains alongside my grandparents before my mother and father moved to the city. Early in our youth, my grandparents showed us how to make a device to ward off any bad spirits or people that may come to our door. And whether it be what we learned to build or not, our homes were always safe from harm. My grandparents had these devices all around their home, even outside. Same with my parents, my brother. We trusted it. And again, maybe it was because of the device, or maybe just faith, or…even luck."

"How does that help our situation?" Logan wondered.

"Because I can build you one and leave it here."

"And what will it do?" Hillary asked.

"It will keep the balance in your home. If there's anything bad or evil here created by the prior owner, it will keep it at bay. Give you no harm. This is what we believe. Are you willing to accept one if I build it for you? I'll even show you how to make it if the one I build would ever break in the future, which I hope is long and happy in this house, and I believe it could be that for you. I don't know what exactly that black is—perhaps it's that eyes-watching-you feeling you have down in the basement, Hillary—but if it is something to worry about, something related to what happened down there, what I give you will keep you, Logan, and your home at peace. The balance restored."

"I'm okay with it," Hillary said eager.

"Me too," Logan continued. "Wouldn't hurt, right? Just in case?"

"Exactly," Gunnar replied. "Just in case. It definitely won't hurt."

"Okay. Build us one," Logan insisted. "What do you need?"

"If you have any thin wire and a leather lace that would be a great start to hold everything together."

"I have some in a toolbox, yes. What else?" Logan asked.

"I need to take a walk through your yard, and it would be quite kind if I could have two roses from that beautiful rose bush you have out front."

Hillary chuckled and walked to the front door. "Why of course. Let's go."

Gunnar followed her while Logan went for the toolbox. He picked out two bloomed red roses, and Hillary snipped them off.

"Can you cut the stem a bit more? I only need a few inches of stem."

Hillary cropped each stem while Gunnar walked to a tree, reaching for a branch. He broke it in two with his hands, each about a foot long. Then he grabbed another, splitting that one as well, giving him four sticks. He walked back to Hillary by the door.

"Got everything?" she asked.

He held up the sticks. "This is all I need."

They walked inside and sat at the table where Logan waited with the lace and thin wire.

"Okay, perfect," Gunnar began. "Again, I'm going to show you so if this ever breaks, you can fix it."

The Masterses both nodded, ready to learn.

Gunnar took the four sticks and the thin wire, wrapping the top. He set them on the table, spreading the sticks apart, each one facing a cardinal direction. With the lace, he wrapped the stems of the roses so they held tightly together with a knot. The other end of the lace went up the center of the sticks. Gunnar weaved it through the sticks and wire. When he got it in his hand, he looped it back down, knotting it to itself. The roses hung upside down and in the center of the four sticks. It looked like some kind of pendulum.

"All righty," Gunnar said. "There you both go. The device that keeps the balance."

"Really?" Logan laughed. "That's it?"

"That's it."

"So now what?" Hillary asked.

"Yeah," Logan furthered. "What should we do with it? I mean, do we put it anywhere? A certain spot in the house?"

"It doesn't have to be anywhere exactly, no. But if you want my opinion, I'd put it somewhere you won't see it every day. That way you don't have to be reminded of why it's here in the first place. Check up on it though from time to time. Make sure it's always upright like this. Make sure the lace hasn't worn or rotted and the sticks haven't fallen away from one another. If so, the balance is once again broken. The roses being suspended upside down will preserve them for quite some time. But eventually they *will* fall apart. Just replace them with new, beautiful ones like outside."

"We're thankful for this, and for you," Logan admitted.

"Yes, thank you. I have a good idea where to put it," Hillary said. She grabbed it gently and left the room.

6.

"SHE PUT IT in the attic, didn't she?" William Cobb asked Gunnar. He got up from his chair and went for the brandy bottle again.

"Yes, sir, she did," Gunnar admitted.

William scoffed. "And let me guess, you're gonna tell me you know—or can *see*—that I found and removed it from the house?"

"It's not that I can see you removing it from the house, it's the simple fact that I can see that blackness again.

I ran this home's Spool when I walked in; I can see you and your daughter moving in. And then just blackness again. The same blackness I saw so long ago. It's here again, because you broke the balance of this house."

William laughed at the man. Brandy filled the bottom of his glass. "I don't believe any of this sort of stuff. You lost me long ago, so please excuse my attitude now. I believe that you were in the circus—you seem crazy enough—and I believe you stayed here based on the pictures you had shown me. Hell, I even believe you built that thing I found in the attic. But I can't trust anything else you've told me. I believe in life and death. Facts. Before buying the home, I was informed of its history. Even if the first owner did have wild orgies in the basement and eventually killed himself during some ritual, I don't believe in any sort of bad energy left behind. Or this 'blackness' you say you see. Christ, it was over fifty years ago. Let it go."

"I think you're being very unwise right now, William."

"And I think you're here only to scare us. For the sake of arguing, let's say you really can see the history of this house. How do you know this blackness never left? Maybe it was still here all this time?"

"It never did leave," Gunnar responded. "But after Hillary Masters put the pendulum in the attic, I kept in contact with both of them. We were pen pals, and would also chat on the phone. They'd assure me things were great with them and likewise with the house. And when the circus the following year was headed back to New York, they invited me to stay with them again. And I did. When I showed up, we all stood in the living room. I ran the Spool of the house.

I saw it *all* again. Then came the blackness. And to my great relief that wasn't the end of the Spool. The blackness faded and I could see Hillary and Logan making memories. The blackness was at bay, abiding to the balance. Coming and staying with them started a routine, and I stayed ever year until I retired. And each year, I ran the Spool of the house, and then each of theirs. The blackness never showed itself back in the history line, anywhere. I believe it was because of the rose pendulum."

"If that thing was so important, why didn't the Masterses take it with them?"

"Because they knew how to build their own, just in case. And more and most importantly: for your protection."

William rolled his eyes.

"When they called and told me last year they would be moving and selling the home, they said they were going to leave it behind for the next homeowners. They moved to Montana, near their daughter, and into assisted living. They weren't getting any younger and wanted to be close to her. While speaking to them, they asked a final favor. If I could keep an eye on the house, see when it sold, and then visit the new owners to make sure the pendulum was still here and safe."

"Ah," William voiced. "So it has been lies from the beginning. You aren't on your way visiting an old friend. You're here on a favor, to search my house. I now think would be a good time for you to leave. You've had your time and said enough."

"Sir, please."

"Enough," William said. "If what you said is true about the Masterses, why wouldn't they just call me themselves?"

"They feared you wouldn't believe them. Or you had changed the landline number."

"Well, I wouldn't have believed them either. They were right. This is all nonsense. Now, I won't ask you again. Please leave. Now. You're done with your voodoo stories and trying to scare me. You're lucky my daughter hasn't heard any of this."

But to everyone's surprise, she had.

"Daddy?" Macy said, stepping out from behind the wall, centered there in the kitchen entrance.

"Macy! What are you doing up? Go back up to bed."

"Are we gonna be okay?" she asked.

"Oh, that does it, old man. Get up and get out! Now! Before I do it myself. And you won't care for that if I do."

Gunnar slid his chair back.

"Again, William, I think this is a bad—"

"You're done talking. You've scared my daughter now. Get out of my house!"

Gunnar put his coat and gloves on and walked past the Cobbs with his umbrella, grabbing his briefcase next to William's recliner. At the front door, Gunnar turned around.

"I wish you both the best of luck."

"Out! Now!"

Gunnar sighed. Looked defeated. Sorrow filled his face as he already began to fear for them. And it was not that he even knew what that blackness was, but it was back, almost as if it were not at bay, but asleep, alive, and waiting for the balance to fall. And it had. Now it was awake again, Gunnar believed—he saw. A veil hiding history, to be absorbed into the house's walls. That sheet of darkness was a power Gunnar did not like, never could trust. He knew he could help like before, but this time he was being sent away, ignored, his name and story labeled as insane. Holding the knob in his hand, Gunnar took a final look at the family, hoping they would be able to hold each other like that for years to come.

He hoped....

Gunnar went back into the rain, opening the umbrella.

William watched from the window.

Gunnar got in a car across the street and drove off in the direction opposite of the hotel where he said he was saying. Where he was going was unknown, but at least he was gone.

"Daddy?" Macy said.

"Yes, dear. What is it?"

"You never answered me. Are we gonna be okay?"

William knelt to his daughter and looked at her directly in the eyes. "Yes, Macy. We're gonna be okay. As long as I'm in this house, you have nothing to worry about."

"Even after all that scary stuff that man said? He said people died in here."

"Yes, honey. There were some people that passed away in here a long time ago. But that doesn't mean it has to scare you. What if mommy would've passed away here in this house and not the other one? Would you think this house would be scary then?"

"I guess not," Macy said.

"So you have no reason to be scared, you see? No different. It happened long, long ago. Please, trust me,

Mace."

"Okay, Daddy. I will. As long as you're here, I know I'll be safe."

"That's right. I promise."

Macy hugged her father, letting him go a second later. She looked at him, puzzled.

"What is it, Macy?"

"Daddy, what are orgies?"

Jesus Christ, William thought.

7.

MACY COULD NOT rest, even if she persuaded William to let her sleep in his bed for the night. He agreed, and she laid there staring at the ceiling, listening to her father's snoring. By six a.m., according to the alarm clock beside her, she did feel exceptionally tired after not sleeping, but she was more so bored and hungry after hours of silence. Also, she did not feel nearly as scared as she was the evening before. There was something comforting in just knowing it was now morning—even if it was quite early and still dark—that helped ease the anxiety that was with her through the dead of night.

She rolled out of bed.

"Mace, what's up?" William asked. "You okay?"

"Yeah, Daddy. Just hungry. Maybe I'll have some cereal and watch cartoons downstairs."

William yawned. "It's Saturday. I don't care," William said tired. "I'm going to stay in bed a bit longer. Can you be a good girl and get the paper for me?"

"Yep."

Macy left the room, kicking on the hallway light, illuminating her path. She went down the stairs and to the front door, turning on the lights there to awaken the living room. She opened the door to find not only the paper, but four sticks and two roses in the center hanging upside down, a similar design to the one she overheard last night from the stranger. She turned around.

William was not there, presumably back to sleep.

There was a small piece of paper under one of the sticks. Macy picked it up and read aloud: "Just in case."

After last night, she knew how her father felt, what he believed. And yes, she did feel safe with him in the house. But what if the stranger in the night was actually truthful? Even though she trusted her father, she had questions now, a small hint of fear, like seeing something that haunts you for a while; you dare not share such emotion so quickly unless your heart fully believes or disbelieves in something. And she did not. Not completely. And if she had questions…that was not true faith.

Macy knelt to the rose pendulum and the newspaper. She took the note out from under the stick, jamming it in her pajama pocket. Picking up both the paper and the pendulum, she quietly walked back inside, desperately trying to keep her father asleep. She feared that if he saw her with the pendulum, he would destroy this one, too, just like he threw the other into the fireplace after bringing it out of the attic.

After putting the newspaper on the recliner, she made her way back up the stairs with the pendulum, so careful, weightless. The roses swayed back and forth between the sticks. Macy paused before her father's door, stretching her neck around the doorframe as far as she could. The roses stopped moving, perfectly centering themselves between the pieces of wood. It was dark in William's room, and she could hear him snoring again. She smiled, that paranoia gone, and walked to her room and shut the door. The pendulum had to be hidden. For the time being, she decided on her closet until the right time would come to put it back in the attic. The attic would probably be the best place for it again. It would be out of sight, away from William, even if the attic was where he found the other one while storing old belongings and relics that had no need to be displayed in the house. Macy's first dresser was up there, boxes of old clothes, William's outdated college books and childhood pictures, et cetera. Since all these things were unneeded, Macy figured her father would have no reason to go back into the attic, at least not for a while. She just had to wait until she was alone, a few minutes by herself. The door that led to the attic was in the spare room, an office-to-be. Macy would surely wake her father, making noise in there and then walking above him.

She went to her closet and placed the pendulum in the back corner where it was darkest, keeping it upright like she heard the night before, and shut the door. Macy made her way back down the steps and turned on the television, sitting on the floor with her toys. The cartoons made her smile, feel good, almost erased her hunger. But she wondered if she felt this way for another reason. A sense of greater safety perhaps? She had her father in the house, and also the pendulum—just in case. She felt okay for the first time since her father put her to bed the night before. Her eyes felt heavy, finally finding sleep, a sort of peace and confidence.

8.

WHEN MACY WOKE, she was still on the living room floor. The television was now off, and the newspaper was missing from the recliner.

Daddy must be up, she thought.

She went into the kitchen and looked out the back door. William was in the yard picking up random sticks that had fallen during the storm. A rake rested against a tree. Macy sprinted back through the kitchen and to the staircase, only to stop in front of her closet doors. She grabbed the pendulum and went to the storage room.

Macy opened the door to the attic and hit the light. A dozen wooden steps greeted her. In the corner of the attic was her old dresser—the one from when she was a baby. It was crimson and had several drawers, all of which, though, were too shallow to place the pendulum. Behind the dresser were a few of her other younger possessions: a tiny rocking chair with her name carved into the top, a stool, boxes filled with old clothes and memories. Macy placed the pendulum on the stool. It stood strong, the roses swaying back and forth before coming to a stop again in the center of the stick formation. She smiled, feeling safe, confident, and sneaky, too. When she made it back to the stairs, Macy turned around, looking at her old dresser. It was all she could see in the spot in the attic; her rocking chair, stool, boxes, and now the pendulum, were out of sight, hidden behind the height of the dresser. She trusted the pendulum would be safe, along with herself and her father.

And for many years, they were, living peacefully, nearly forgetting about the stranger in the night and the pendulum altogether.

9.

A PHONE RANG in William Cobb's house.

"Hello?" William answered.

"Hi, Dad."

"Why hello, dear. How are you today?"

"I'm doing really well. Thank you. I'm calling you to tell you the good news," Macy said.

"Oh yeah? What are you gonna tell me? You finally found a decent man and are gonna bless me with some grandchildren before I keel over?"

Macy laughed into the phone. "I think I got something better."

"Must be good then. Let's hear it."

"I just got done talking to my supervisor. She offered me a new job."

"That *is* exciting, yes. Is it a promotion?"

"Yes, and a relocation."

He groaned. "Not sure if I like that, Mace," William began, "you're already four hours away from me."

"But you didn't let me finish. They're transferring me back home. Well, over the mountain to the hospital in Blakesview. I'll be working in the new pharmaceutical department they built last year. Can you believe it? After all these years away from you and home, I can come back and be closer. I'm so excited!"

And she was. Macy had left her father's home shortly after graduating high school, immediately planting herself into college, and has been hours away ever since, living in a small rental close to work for the past decade. She had come home mainly for holidays, a couple days maximum. This was a void she had always hoped to refill one day, to see him more throughout the year. And the day had now come, even if it took until the year 2018.

"You're right," William said. "This is better than a grandchild. At least right now. Maybe you can work on that when you're back and settled?"

"Dad…"

"I know, I know. I'll stop. So…when's this happening? Is work gonna help you find a place to live or you on your own with that?"

"They're gonna help me move my belongings to wherever I find a place to live. And for that, I'm thankful. Saves me a lot of money and hassle. I start over the mountain in a month. So I'll be seeing you very soon. Just got to find a nice little apartment in the meantime."

"This is wonderful, Mace. Just in time for Thanksgiving and Christmas. That's always been your favorite time of year. Maybe you can help me with some of the decorating this year? Your old man isn't getting any younger. I have an idea though. I know you're a grown woman, but why don't you come and stay with me until you find a suitable place to live? I know it'll be a small hike over the mountain to commute, but…it'll save you some bucks until then. What do you say? Be great to have you in the house again. Been lonely for many years."

"That's 'cause you never found anyone as good as Mom."

"Well, you aren't lying about that, are ya?"

Macy smirked into the phone. "Well, Dad, I guess

as long as you say it's okay to stay with you, I'll do that. Sure. It'll be good to be home."

"You're my daughter. You're always welcome here with me. I'll have your room nice and clean and ready."

"I know, Dad. Thank you. But I better get going now. My break's about over, but I rushed to the phone when they told me the news. I wanted you to know right away."

"And I'm so glad you did. I'm thrilled to hear this."

"Me, too. See you soon, Dad. I love you."

"Love you, too, Macy. Glad you're coming home."

10.

"MY GOODNESS DO those cookies smell good," William said to his daughter as he came up from the basement. His coat was in the dryer, as he had been shoveling the sidewalks in front of the house a couple of hours before.

"And you can't touch them until they cool," Macy returned, smiling as she put another rack of raw dough and chocolate chips into the oven. "You going back out?"

William looked out the window. The corner streetlight illuminated the intersection, streaming with the glitter of the falling snow. It was shortly after seven in the evening, and both their bodies were filled with supper and warmth from William's "famous" chili and the fireplace throwing off heat. The interior of the house was welcoming the Christmas season; a decorated tree stood tall in the living room, and many strings of lights weaved through the bushes and hung like pulsing, sparkling icicles off the rain gutters.

"Yeah, I better. Gotta try and keep up with it. Less work for the morning. Doesn't look like they hit the roads in a while. Figures. What are you gonna do while those cookies cook?"

Macy hummed. "You know what? Maybe I'll finally go through a couple of those boxes in the attic. I'd like to find this board game, if you'd want to play. Thank you again for putting them up there, along with all my other things I haven't used since I've been home."

"I didn't put them up there," William laughed. "I just told the movers where to put the stuff that would fit up there. I must say, though, I do like the couch in the basement. Maybe I'll turn that into a little den one day. And yes, let's play a game when I get back in. I'd like that."

Macy smiled and removed her apron as her father went out the door.

When her feet connected with the attic stairs, she stopped, absorbing the memories of the select few times she ever went up these stairs. God, how long had it been? Even during the entirety of her youth, it was rare—less than a handful of times a year—when she or her father would use the attic. The corridors were nearly unused since moving there, aside from William getting the Christmas decorations and artificial tree once a year, and placing Macy's school papers and report cards in a designated box. Most of the Cobbs belongings instead gathered dust in the basement.

I wonder if it's still up here, Macy thought to herself. *Unless Dad found and tossed it like the other one.*

She doubted it, though. William had never brought it up. However, it had been many years since Macy herself last saw the pendulum, checking on it before leaving for college some sixteen years ago. That was the only reason she even went up to the attic when she was growing: to check on it. Even when visiting her father throughout the year, she did not bother. There simply was no time or even a desire to do such a thing during her short stays. Plus, there never was a problem with the house, always so peaceful, loving, harmless as it should have been. Her father safe.

She got to the landing and turned left, making her way back to where her old dresser stood strong. And behind it, there it was, the pendulum, still together, balanced and standing on an old stool. The two roses were beyond dry and brittle. The sticks had collected a thick layer of dust like most other things around them. Macy lightly pushed the roses, testing the leather lace. They swayed back and forth for a moment before stopping back in the center of the sticks.

"Unbelievable," Macy said to herself, chuckling. "Better to just leave it be, just in case." She stood back up and turned away.

A second later, from outside, she heard her neighbor, Phillip Deadman, scream: "William! WATCH OUT!"

The house shook something awful immediately after. A vibration ran through every inch of the place. Macy dropped to her knees, catching herself. She heard other things fall inside the house. She turned and looked back at the pendulum. It was on the floor now. The roses practically burst into dust. The sticks were close by, separated and loose, the wire no longer holding them tightly together.

An odd sense of anxiety started to crawl within her—a superstition created when she was a child.

"WILLIAM!" Macy heard for a second time.

His name gave her energy again and she rushed down the steps, slamming the door behind her, ignoring—

forgetting—the pendulum altogether.

What was wrong with her father?

As she made her way to the front door, she passed picture frames and knickknacks on the floor, broken, and several Christmas bulbs that had fallen off the tree from the jolt that went through the house. She opened the front door in a frenzy, and there stood Phillip.

"Dear God, Macy. You can't see this."

"What?! What happened? Where's Dad?" She noticed there were slide marks in the yard leading to the side of the house, caused by something she did not know. Or did she know and just did not want to believe it? She stepped forward.

"No, Macy. Don't."

"Let me go," Macy returned, smelling alcohol on him, tearing herself from Phillip's half-drunk grip. She jumped off the porch and scurried to the side of the house, following the marks in the snow. Macy dropped to her knees a moment later and screamed holy agony when she saw both her father and the origin of the slices in the snow.

A car had come through the yard, pinning William to the side of the house. Blood from his mouth created a small pool on the car's hood. Snow continued to fall around him, and sparking lights blinked above and beside his body.

She wanted to run but could not. She wanted for him to come inside and play a game, but he could not. She wanted this to be a dream, but it was not. She wanted his eyes to open, his mouth to speak, but they could not.

It was Phillip Deadman who had given both police and Macy a full description of what had happened. Phillip was on his porch sipping a whiskey after finishing shoveling his own sidewalk. He and William had a quick conversation, yelling across the yard to one another until Phillip let him get to work. While sitting there, he turned as he heard a car coming—cresting the hill. He watched the headlights appear, but they did not stop—and typically, for this time of year, *anyone* who knew about this hill and its reputation knew to come to a near-stop before trying to come down in the road when it was snow-covered. There had been countless accidents of cars sliding into parked cars over the years. William, Macy, Phillip, and nearly everyone else who had lived on this block had seen it happen. He sipped his drink and watched, laughing quietly to himself when the car swerved after hitting the brakes.

"Oh, here we go," Phillip said into his glass.

A flash of red colored the landscape behind the car. The car gracefully went broadside in the center of the road, missing all other vehicles until facing forward again.

"Keep it together there, bud," Phillip continued.

William did not hear Phillip over the grinding of his metal shovel on the concrete. The car continued straight in the middle of the road, unable to see the center line, gaining speed down the hill—a speed that created a heat inside of Phillip aside from the signature warmth of whiskey. He knew he was going too fast. Even covered with thick material, it was undeniable that his hands and forehead started to sweat, waiting for something to happen.

"You're better off chancing it now and go barreling through the intersection. Don't jerk that wheel again, pal. Or hit the brakes."

The car continued to roll more rapidly until two stray cats ran out across the street, playing. The driver instinctively jammed the brakes right in front of Phillips home. The car slid wildly, no indication of stopping, at least not organically. It hopped the curb in front of William's house and came ripping through the yard.

"WILLIAM! WATCH OUT!" Phillip screamed to his neighbor.

William looked up, saw the danger before him, and tried to run. He slipped on the walk, putting his chest at the correct level for the car's hood. And it connected, only to stop after hitting the house, crushing William and the hearts of several nearby.

11.

WILLIAM'S WILL HAD left both money and the house to Macy. She hated the idea—let alone the physical act—of staying there. The house held sorrow and memories, nothing more, for she knew that would be all she would ever have now. For months, as she would drive home from work, her mind would repress the idea of even seeing the house, seeing the exact corner where her father was killed. It did nothing but bring her down further into a hole when she thought her feet had already touched the bottom. But lonesomeness is a never-ending gateway, is it not, unless some happiness could eventually be found.

And Macy had, even if it was not in the sanest of ways. Approximately three months after William's death was when she knew she was not entirely alone in the house. Up until that time, she would hear small noises while in the house, often footsteps upstairs by her father's room. Of course, this had startled Macy initially. But the more it happened, the more she believed it was just her father in the house, still looking after her, keeping to his word he said to her the night the stranger left: "As long as I'm in this house, you'll be safe."

As time went on and these unexplained occurrences multiplied, her depression started to evaporate, feeling okay and safe again in the house. Not only were the events happening more often, but they were becoming stronger, more…personal and precise. There were times she could smell him; a smell engraved into her mind since she had only known her father to ever wear a single kind of cologne. And in the months of June through August, together they had played an entire chess game. Macy would move a piece and say aloud that it was her father's turn. Some mornings an opposing piece would be moved; other mornings not. All of the experiences had finally brought up Macy's courage to go into the attic and dig out some old photographs of William. Until then, she had doubted she could look at his face and not cry. But it had been months of dry eyes; only a sense of happiness back in her heart.

When she got to the landing of the attic, she remembered then the last time she was in there: the night of the accident.

"The pendulum," she said to herself.

The thought of it was all but completely absent until then. The initial depression of William's death had stifled the memory of it shattering, for a hurt mind and heart will erase all forms of reminiscence aside from what aches the soul. And even after the interactions began, Macy was distracted by the contentment refilling her life, even if she knew William would never return through the door. But she believed he was there still in some special kind of way.

She neglected looking for the box of old pictures and went back to her old dresser. Behind it was the stool where the pendulum once stood. She looked at the floor at the spot where she had seen it last when it fell. But there was nothing, only a spread of dust. It was missing. Every piece.

"Dad?" Macy said slow. "Did you finally find it and take it away again?" She smiled and looked around, knowing her father had the ability to move objects. But where did he put it? "I had it hid up here for so many years. I'm sorry."

The attic door slammed shut just then, scaring her.

Macy then shyly laughed once her heart settled. "I guess so then, huh? You did find it. That silly old man wasn't the one trying to protect us. It has always been you, Dad. You were the one who kept us safe. Not that thing."

The attic door then reopened without effort or reason.

12.

THE INTERACTIONS CONTINUED for another year and a half, until it was just days shy of the anniversary of William's death. Each time the experiences would touch Macy's heart, keeping her feeling safe, not alone. However, she was growing more vulnerable, becoming a soft sponge of emotion, opening her up for a potentially deeper hurt if William stopped making his presence known. Perhaps she was not entirely grasping reality as she should have been; she was moving on with her life, but not entirely, not accepting William was gone because it never felt as such.

The interior of the house was once again filled with color and Christmas decorations, and Macy had pulled a cookie sheet out from the oven. As they cooled, she got ready for bed, smelling her father as she passed his room. She smiled, and when she got back to the kitchen she paused. One of the kitchen cabinets had been opened, and a plate sat by the sink with three cookies already on them. She had never seen this before, even last Christmas. Was he getting stronger?

"Now, Dad. You know they have to cool."

There was no sort of response through the Christmas classics playing on the radio, which she turned off a moment later and listened. Still nothing. Would the three cookies be gone in the morning? If so, where? Just like the pendulum—the pieces were never found. Perhaps the same would happen with the cookies? She did not know, but she knew she would find out in the morning.

"Good night, Dad," Macy said, leaving the kitchen. She went up the stairs and passed his room. No scent this time. She shrugged and went into her bedroom, closing the door behind her.

And four hours later, it reopened.

A screech—a familiar sound from her childhood coming forward in her mind—entered Macy's room. Macy batted her eyes, slowly coming awake. She rolled over and sat partially upright in bed, noticing the door now open, the hallway light visible.

"Dad?" Macy softly questioned, because she had not known her father to disrupt her while she slept, whether William was dead or alive. She waited, but the room was still, silent. If anything, Macy started to notice a sour, toilet smell in her room, but it was categorically unrecognizable, foreign. She wrinkled her nose.

"What is that?"

"*Me*," something whispered—something close to a male's voice hidden beneath layers and layers of unseen thickness generated by reality and living time.

Macy froze yet was surely awake now, questioning the origin of the voice and if it was benign. The only thing she knew was that it was *not* her father, and yet, she questioned because what else—who else—could it possibly be?

"Dad?" Macy repeated, shaking, feeling herself grow weak, filling with paranoia and wonder and fear. "Daddy?" she whimpered childishly.

The lights instantly came on.

Macy screamed.

"It's not Daddy; Daddy's not here; Daddy's not allowed here," the voice said.

Was it slightly louder that time? Perhaps due to the energy in the light?

The lights went out, then immediately back on.

"It's not Daddy; Daddy's not here; Daddy's not allowed here."

Absolutely louder that time.

The lights went out. On again.

"It's not Daddy; Daddy's not here."

Macy screamed. "Who are you?!"

The lights went into a frenzy, flickering on and off.

"IT'S NOT DADDY! DADDY'S NOT HERE! IT'S NOT DADDY! DADDY'S NOT HERE!"

Sparks shot from the electrical outlets; the energy taken elsewhere. Two sticks came flying through the doorway at her, each one scraping her face.

The sticks from the pendulum?

They hit the wall behind her and levitated, creating an inverted cross. Macy turned back, and two more sticks came in her direction. These she ducked. They hit the wall and did the same thing. Each caught on fire, and the walls quickly turned bright, dancing with flame.

"IT'S NOT DADDY! DADDY'S NOT HERE! IT'S NOT DADDY! DADDY'S NOT HERE! IT'S NOT DADDY! DADDY'S NOT HERE!"

Macy continued to scream in horror, and then all three windows in her room exploded, sending glass into the yard. She covered herself and her ears. She looked at the doorway. It was vacant.

But was it?

Chance it.

Quickly, Macy jumped to the floor and went for the door, but something grabbed her, tripping her to the ground. It was the corner of the bedsheet; it was wrapped around her ankle, coiling, constricting like a snake. She stepped on the sheet with her other leg and yanked, freeing herself, sprinting to the hallway.

She thought about jumping the railing, chancing a tall drop into the edge of the living room, but she did not. Macy raced to the staircase. On the way, each outlet popped, catching the wall ablaze, and by the sound of it, every one of them downstairs did, too. Even in the basement?

Halfway down the steps, she dramatically stopped, sliding down several. She gazed in terror. Finally, she could see it. Enough energy had been consumed by the popping outlets to manifest what was causing all of this. And it was nothing but an absolute massive blackness.

It moved quickly through the doorway of the kitchen, wrapping its dark waving sheets against the living room walls, pushing itself forward. It had no definition, no shape, just an incredible phantasm that tested the height of the house as it touched the ceiling and started to contour to its shape, still growing.

Macy could not scream, only think. *Was this what the stranger in the night saw? That blackness he warned us about? The blackness that he didn't know or why it was there. What he saw wasn't blocking his vision; what he saw was* this *entity in the house, waiting. Was this what I thought was Dad? Was it mocking me, imitating him, using our bond to work on me? Make me weak? Vulnerable? Was Dad never here? Only this?*

The walls continued to burn, and the thing started to move, like someone pulling a curtain across the entire room, perhaps trying to block Macy's exit. The front door was not too far, but it was going to be a race.

She clenched her teeth, rushing to the bottom of the stairs. The curtain was so fast, keeping up with her. Macy screamed and pushed herself harder until she knew she was going to collide with the blackness. She noticed it looked partially transparent the longer it stretched on. Could she jump through it, make it to the door?

Screaming, she leaped and closed her eyes, waiting to hit the floor again through the black curtain.

When she felt her feet touch the ground, she opened her eyes again and had no ambition to run. Surrounding her was a vast darkness, completely crippling any understanding where she was or how much space this place occupied.

A scream nearby startled her. She turned, and turned again, once more. There was no way to tell where it had come from. Then another scream, and another. The sound of…loud chewing followed. Was something eating? Macy shook, wondering where she was exactly, the possibility that she was getting the answer to who or what this blackness was. Was this where it rightfully belonged? In the dark? Creating screams. Maybe feeding? The choir of sickening sounds only got louder. Macy yelled against it. And as she did so, she noticed the effect; the black walls were melting hearing her, creating a sort of disturbance, perhaps due to the fact she did not *belong* there, and her emotion altered that area's space and time. She took a deep breath and roared again, and slowly her living room was coming back into view until she was on the floor, surrounded by smoke and fire.

Macy got to her feet feeling terribly weak. Her vision was blurred. Or was she seeing several of the same thing? Which door was the correct one to exit? She rushed ahead, stumbling on the way to the multiple front doors. Macy reached for a knob, feeling warm metal in her hand; got it correct first try. She turned it and thrust herself onto the porch, sliding down the steps and finally resting in the snow.

Phillip Deadman rushed to her, freeing his jacket on the way.

13.

MACY SIGHED AS she rested in her hospital bed after reliving the night before and her youth.

Officer Risper finished writing, finally. He absorbed—was processing—what he had heard. He folded the pad over and looked at Macy. "I think that you're quite lucky to be alive."

"You don't believe me, do you?"

He hummed. "I do believe you were attacked, Macy. That evidence is quite clear. But I can't do anything against the paranormal. We need facts and evidence. Always. I'm not saying I could never believe in ghosts—I've had some odd encounters, too—but I've never been able to justify my superstitions. And even so, there's no one to arrest, because no one can be tried. I need a person. And I believe a person did this to you. If something continued to yell at you like you say...that was no ghost. I'm sorry."

"What about what I saw? The blackness I went through. How do you explain that? The sticks, and the outlets catching fire. My windows exploded, for Christ's sake."

"Easy, Macy. The blackness could've easily been smoke. Your mind created things during such an experience. You were probably inhaling smoke, not knowing it until your brain processed it. You passed out on the floor and had a terrible dream until coming to again. Thankfully for you, you did. The sticks, I don't know. Perhaps someone threw them up at you. As far as them sticking to the wall and turning into inverted crosses, that I can't explain, and you can't either. You could've been delirious from the stress and smoke inhalation. Maybe there has been a short in the house causing the sockets to do what you say they did. Heat easily could've broken the windows."

"They *exploded*," Macy hissed to his ignorance.

"Even if this were all true, Macy, what could I do?"

She looked the other way.

"The best thing—and if I may add, the correct and right way to do this—is to think who would do this to you? Someone was in the house saying those things to you. Trying to scare you. So...think, Macy. Think. Who could possibly want to do this to you?"

"No one."

"Come—"

"No one, I said."

The policeman shook his head. "I think I should let you rest. I'll take back what I've gathered from our talk and my notes and think about what we should do next—how we can get this son of a bitch."

"You're leaving?!" Macy gasped.

"I have to, Macy. I have a family at home. I'll come back tomorrow and check up on you. Maybe I'll have some more questions. Or perhaps answers after talking further with the fire department and investigators."

"But, but..."

"What, Macy?"

"What if that thing followed me? It wanted me. Grew close to me. And I let it."

"I don't know what you want me to say to that. I think it was a person who did this to you. And if it makes you feel better, I'll call my higher-up and see if I can have him send in someone to look after you tonight. Stay outside the door. If anyone has followed you, Macy, it would be a person. And so, I'd be very much okay with having someone look after your room tonight. Would that be okay? Enough?"

Macy tossed her hands. "I guess so."

"Do you want someone here or not? If it would make you feel better, I can recommend it, and I'll stay here until they arrive."

Macy nodded slowly and looked away.

14.

"MACY," OFFICER RISPER said, "this is Officer Harris."

"Hi, Macy," Harris said.

Macy shyly smiled. "Hi."

"Very sorry to hear what happened to you and your home. But I'll be right outside the door if you need anything. Well, anything that I can provide. Afraid I won't be much help with anything medically." His humor was terrible and yet he laughed to himself.

"I'll come by tomorrow, okay?" Risper said.

"Don't know what good it'll be; I told you everything," Macy replied.

"Well, just to check on you. And like I said, maybe I'll have another question. But hopefully answers. Get your rest, Macy. Thanks for telling me everything."

Both officers left the room, closing the door.

"Mind if I get your phone number?" Risper asked Harris. "In case I think of something on the way home or later today, I can give you a call and you can communicate to her for me."

"Of course."

Risper went to the elevator. Harris sat on a bench across the hall from Macy's room.

Macy laid there, staring at the ceiling, thinking of

the hell of what happened and not being believed. She was tired after such a tale and slowly closed her eyes.

An unknown warmth started below her, and she questioned if, perhaps, an air vent was kicking out heat; it was winter in a hospital, after all. It continued to make itself known in the room, crawling up the side of her bed, stimulating her arms. It felt wonderful, calm. It rose to her face, and when it swam under her nose, her eyes instantly opened against a faint stench. Something sour. The ceiling was crawling with black, nearly vibrating; the sides of her bed were waving darkness. Macy went to scream, but there was a solid smear of blackness across her lips, stopping her, choking her as it went into her mouth and down her throat.

With the door closed, no one saw a thing…

15.

"GODDAMMIT," RISPER SAID to himself, patting his pockets in an overexaggerated manner. "Forgot my keys again." He thought back, remembering his keys on the stand beside Macy's bed. Digging for his phone, he called Harris.

"Think of something already?" Harris asked, answering the phone.

Risper smirked. "No. I forgot my keys. They're beside Macy's bed. Would you mind getting them for me. I'll meet you halfway. Save me a partial trip. Would ya?"

"No problem. Hang on a bit and make sure I find them. You said beside Macy?"

"Yes."

"Okay." Harris stood up and went to her door,

opening it. "Macy!" Harris yelled.

Risper listened, curious.

"Sit down. Get back in bed!" Harris demanded.

"Harris? What the hell's going on?" Risper demanded into the phone.

"It's Macy. She's jumping up and down on the bed. Something doesn't seem—"

Macy then leapt at him.

The phone dropped to the floor, creating an awful noise in Risper's ear.

"Harris? Harris? Talk to me."

Breathing came through the phone.

"Harris? Tell me what's going on."

The breathing continued, and a small female laugh came through.

"Macy?"

It continued to breathe, faster, more manic.

"Macy? Is that you?"

"It's not Macy; Macy's not here. It's not Macy; Macy's not here."

Risper's heart almost exploded with fear and...belief. He jammed the phone in his pocket and burst through the hospital doors. There were people already making their way to the elevator and stairwell. Risper took the stairs, jumping multiple at a time, gun in hand. He hit the fourth floor and bolted to the crowd outside Macy's room.

"Move!" Risper demanded. He rounded the corner and stopped dead.

Harris's clothes had nearly been torn off, and blood continued to make its way across the floor as Macy chewed through Harris's neck.

He was certainly dead; his head was barely hanging on.

Risper denied the initial instinct to vomit.

"Macy!" Risper screamed.

She whipped her head towards him. A dark red covered her face up to the bridge of her nose with several streaks on her forehead. She chewed a second more and swallowed what was in her mouth. The sound echoed the room, sickening Risper more.

"Stop, Macy. I believe you now," Risper said.

She snarled, sniffing the air, perhaps considering him next.

"Look, Macy. I'm gonna put my gun down, but you need to step away from Harris. He's gone. You've done enough."

"Never enough," she hissed. "Always hungry." She turned for another mouthful.

"No!" Risper screamed. "Look at me."

She did, baring teeth of red.

"I'm putting my gun down. I'm gonna come over there to you and place these on you? Okay?" Risper questioned holding a pair of cuffs in his hand. He knelt to the floor, putting the gun beside him. He slowly moved forward, seconds between each step.

"Very good, Macy. Very good."

"Oh, forget this! She killed a police officer," a random onlooker said and came pushing forward, grabbing Risper's pistol.

"Don't you dare!" Risper said.

The gun fired regardless....

Most everyone screamed, shielding themselves.

The bullet connected with the center of Macy's chest.

The man dropped the gun and ran through the crowd.

Risper didn't bother and instead went to Macy, who was bleeding out on the floor beside Harris. He held her in his arms.

"Thank you," she said, choking. "Thank you for coming back."

As she died in his arms, he could not help but notice an odd warmth, as if collecting her heat.

A transferring....

The security guards and other policemen on duty at the hospital were dealing with the random shooter who had been tackled by a male nurse in the hall not far from Macy's room.

16.

RISPER LEFT THE hospital as soon as he felt Macy's heart stop, walking passed everyone still in the hall-way. He seemed blank yet...determined. He drove home as fast as he could, his head full of imagery and horror from moments before. He wanted nothing more than to be home, and so he neglected to go to the station, and ignored all phone calls and radio communications from them during his twenty-minute commute. But more so, he did not care. Work could wait, he passively figured, and furthermore, he had this incredible hunger in his stomach. It was the only thing he could concentrate on, a craving, an untouchable de-sire he never knew existed before.

When he walked into his house, his wife was surprised to hear him so early, even if the station had phoned her, saying he may or may not be on his way there. She had her doubts but...here he was.

She called him by name from the upstairs bedroom, where she waited with her two children, asking him to join them, for they had missed him all afternoon.

"Right, kids?" she asked.

They cheered together.

"Also, honey," his wife began, "you may want to check in with the station. They called here looking for you but wouldn't tell me why or what for. They said I better hear it from you. What happened today at the hospital? Is everything okay, Shawn?"

But this was not Shawn Risper anymore; Shawn Risper was not there....

"MOTHER'S PETALS"

SEVERAL STREAMS OF tears traveled down the son's face. And drip by drip, each one landed in the bouquet of flowers he grasped in his hand, mainly filled with white roses. Small blue flowers interlocked within the ivory blossoms, their identity unknown to the son.

He looked down at his mother.

She looked peaceful, eyes closed, resting in her eternal box. She was ready to be fed to the depths of the earth, ready to become food for the ones that crawl under our feet—the ones with many legs and eyes, compensating for their lack of size. The boy laid the flowers on the casket, removing one of the white roses to take home with him.

There was a choice; he could watch if he wanted to, and there was the option to not look as his mother was lowered into the ground. But he did, in fact, witness the event of her being dropped below the earth's surface by the caretakers. This image, he expected, would haunt him, an impression not easily shaken for the rest of his life.

After the meal at the church, the son drove home. Walking in, he still had the rose in his hand, the ache in his heart, his eyes still wet, his vision blurred. He did not know how long the remaining tears in his eyes would last; everyone mourns in different speeds.

The son walked into his favorite room: his study, where books lined the walls. He stopped shortly after entering the doorway. There was a shelf to the right of him, filled with antiques passed down through the family line. He placed the rose from the cemetery on the shelf, slowly putting it down, as if letting it go would eliminate the memory of his mother, but that was surely not the case....

Crying, he turned to leave the room, just as quickly as he entered.

But there was a voice nearby.

It was something so familiar.

The son turned back around, but his mother was not in the room, even if it was her voice he had surely heard.

Listening, the son waited.

"I'm in the rose," the voice said, coming to life again.

The son's heart sank, telling himself that this was merely a trick, a hallucination of grief. And yet...it was a way to hear his mother beyond death, that ache in his heart closing, for now; it was a way to be with her again.

Almost....

He walked to the rose, staring at it as he became eye-level with it on the shelf.

"Mother?" he asked.

"Yes, my son. I'm here," the rose said.

The son saw the petals vibrate as she spoke.

"Please, don't leave me yet," said the rose. "I'm not quite ready to be alone."

"Nor am I," said the son. "Will you always be here?"

"No, my boy. I won't. So go and pull up a chair and enjoy this limited time we have."

"JUST ABOVE THE CHIN"

1.

NOW, I....

Christ, give me a second to collect the correct words. It's been a long time since I've spoken of this story, even though the memory is a nightmare and a living hell that's guaranteed to show its presence at some point during my daily existence, still, even if it is my oldest, living memory. Can you imagine? Your first memory being the worst experience of your life. It's haunting and inescapable, mainly the gulping noises I spontaneously hear in my head, or that certain anxiety I felt when they came across the room, not to mention the words that were whispered in my ear, that unforgettable smell of rot on their breath. And after the several decades of reminders, I don't see those reminders stopping any time soon. An eternal recollection, I'm sure, and for that, I'm sorry for myself, which only makes me selfish because I was spared that night. And why was I saved? For being superstitious; that's the only answer I have. Yes, superstitious—and I'm still superstitious, still doing what saved me, even if I've never heard any cases like my own since. But sometimes, I guess, fiction and the impossible happen and it's better to be safe than sorry.

I'm still not exactly sure what it was that came into the house that night; my eyes were pinned so tightly, scared to death, so I didn't see anything but the darkness inside my mind and the images my running imagination created while I waited for it all to end. But I still think they were vampires.

I know it sounds absurd, so…go ahead and laugh it up, call me ridiculous. I'll wait….

2.

IT WAS MY brother, Neil, who had introduced me to my first dead body during a summer vacation away from school. Some were completely smeared with blood, some were missing various body parts, some had unrecognizable features. I was only seven; Neil was twelve. I looked up to my brother, and despite our age gap, he included me in some of the activities he and his friends would do in our basement while our single mother was away, working her second job until eleven, usually rolling in the door closer to midnight. Neil was my babysitter during such times. Mom had a strict bedtime schedule with me, but Neil always said I could continue to hang and stay up late with the big boys just as long as I didn't tell our mother what we were up to: watching horror movies, and sometimes I would even see them drinking beer that someone snuck from their home and brought into ours. I kept my mouth stapled, though, wanting to continue to be invited by my brother, wanting to still be the "cool little brother." And I was, for a while.

The movies started to give me nightmares. I would never tell my mother why, though, what the source was, why I was getting them; I wanted to keep staying up late with my brother and his pals. After a week or so of straight nightmares, I finally confessed to my mother I was having them, asking her if she knew any way to stop them, fearing they wouldn't at the rate I was going. She looked at me, sorrowfully, thinking of the right words. My mother always had little phrases that would…ease the fear in certain situations, especially for me at a young age. Before she left for work that morning she said, "I know I won't be home to tuck you in, but do me a favor, try something for me. Right before you close your eyes to go to sleep, say these words: 'I am in bed, and I am safe. No matter where my dreams may take me tonight, home again is where I will always wake.' Try that, and see if it helps you. It may not cure the bad dreams—we all get them throughout the year, even me—but maybe if you tell yourself this before bed, it will make you realize that no matter how scary dreams can be, you always come home. And I promise that eventually you will dream of something else, many more things that are more pleasant." She smiled and kissed me softly before leaving for work. That night, I did say those words my mother recited. And oddly, the bad dreams didn't happen. Or at least I didn't remember them upon waking. All I knew was I was home, and I was okay. She was right. The dreams came back to me periodically, I remember, but I never again woke in a panic, just as long as I said those words. It calmed my body, I think, before sleeping, giving me peace about the subconscious journey I was about to take. I still say those words before I go to sleep; some habits are hard to break, especially if they have served you well.

The more movies I watched with Neil, the more immune I was getting to anything horror-related on the screen. The monsters were all too…ridiculous? Almost laughable, because surely nothing of the like would ever happen in our reality. I was understanding that, which helped with the nightmares. They slowed. However, it was the movies about people who were evil that worried me more. It made me realize anyone around me could've been as harmful, sinister. And after seeing my first vampire movie, I feared them the most. They were able to present themselves as human but had the ability of master magicians, able to transform, disappear, not to mention kill. I knew vampires were another creation formed from nothing more than the imagination, nothing to fear, but still…they were too close to human and made me wonder if there actually could be a possibility of such things. The slight consideration. How could anyone know? Vampires were not obvious like giant bugs, or werewolves that clearly would never present themselves in our world. But vampires? Who could be a hundred percent sure?

3.

MOM PICKED ME up from the elementary school, as usual, waiting outside the front doors with the other parents.

"How was your day, sweets?" she asked me.

I thought a moment. "It was okay. Boring. But Tiffany's mom came in with cupcakes and chips. I had a chocolate one with orange icing."

"Aw," Mom voiced. "That sounds nice. And appropriate for Halloween. Just a week away, and same with trick-or-treat night." She smiled. "Speaking of which, I need to go back over to that Halloween store across town for a costume, same place we got your pirate outfit. I had nearly forgotten about our Halloween night coming up at the nursing home. I'm not entirely happy or thrilled about it, but..." Mom paused, thinking, "...but it makes the residents smile. It's for them. I shouldn't be selfish. That okay if we stop quick?"

Was there really an option?

The Halloween store was just as I remembered from the week before when me, Neil, and Mom stopped for our trick-or-treat costumes: thousands of props and attire for the season, spooky music coming from every corner of the building, employees dressed liked images I had seen from movies.

"I need something more fun and cheerful than scary for the residents at the home. What do you think?"

I shrugged. "Clowns are pretty funny," I said.

Mom bobbed her head, acknowledging. "Yeah, a clown suit. I think that's a good idea. Let's see." Mom took my hand and walked me up and down several aisles before she found one to her liking, checking the tags on each. Finally, she picked one. "This should do," she said, looking at the model printed on the plastic. "Oh, the things we do at the home for the people."

We smiled at one another.

"Ready to go?"

I nodded.

We walked up to the counter and stood there for about a minute before my mother started to get impatient. No one was there. She tapped the bell near the register three times. A small door behind the register opened and a man—a man dressed as a vampire—appeared. Honestly, my heart dropped when I saw him and his outfit. My questioning began in full swing again. I studied him. He was much older than the other employees in the building, probably close to fifty. His face was terribly pale, perhaps even painted, and his clothes were black and much too long. And when he said hello his teeth were more yellow than white, except for the two fangs on either side of his mouth. Those were redder, sharper, and hopefully made of plastic.

"My apologies, miss," the man said to my mother. "Had an important phone call to take."

"No problem," my mother replied.

"Will this be it today then? Just the clown costume?"

"Yes. That'll do it for today," my mother said, digging in her purse for her wallet.

"Very well," he said. "I must warn you, though."

My mother's eyes went back to the man. "I'm sorry?"

"This costume is solely just that. If you want the whole getup, may I recommend getting some face paint over there on the rack." The man pointed to his right.

Mom sighed. "Guess I need that to be a clown."

The man smiled at my mother. "Yes, I guess so."

"Honey, stand right here. Don't move. I'll be right back."

"Okay, Mom," I said.

She left my side.

I tried to look busy, tried to look like I was inspecting the store, but all I could feel was this set of eyes on me. It was such a noticeable feeling that I couldn't focus on anything else.

"Do you like vampires?" the man said to who I

guessed was me, even though I was not looking at him—or anyone, for that matter.

Slowly, I twisted my head around. Sure enough, the man was staring at me, smiling hideously.

"Do you like vampires?" he repeated once we were looking at one another.

"No," I said softly. "I don't."

The man nearly frowned. "And may I ask why? Are we too scary?"

"No," I repeated. "It's because you aren't scary at all. Vampires almost look like normal people."

That smile began to appear again on the man's face. "Oh, yes," the man started, "vampires very much look like you or me. They are slick, smart…magical. Aren't they? Can transform themselves and enter your home."

I nervously nodded, practically feeling my body get colder.

"Almost can't tell whether someone's a vampire before it's too late. But I know a trick," he finished, winking.

I squinted at him.

"Oh, yes. There's a trick to protect yourself from vampires. And it's even easier than wearing wreaths of garlic like you may have seen in movies. Do you want to know what it is?"

"So…vampires are real?" I timidly questioned.

"Who can truly be sure, right?"

Exactly, I thought. *Exactly.*

"It would be better to know the trick than to not know it, correct?

I nodded my head quicker. "Yes, yes. Hurry and tell

me. Mom's coming back."

"Okay, sonny. Listen up. This is quite easy like I said. All you have to do is this: before you finally fall asleep at night, just make sure you have your blanket pulled up and over your neck, right above your chin. Hold it there. Hold it there all night long. If you have your neck protected, the vampires can't get you. Can't suck on your blood."

"Sorry, sweets," Mom said as she finished walking up to us. Couldn't make up my mind." She put down a palette of face paint and again went for her wallet, counting.

At the register, the man punched in the prices for both items, giving her a total. They thanked one another. Mom and I started towards the doors, ready to go home. I turned around and looked at the cashier a final time. He smiled wide at me, then raised his clenched hands to the bottom of his chin, as if he were holding an invisible blanket in front of him.

My body shook a moment, then I went back for my mother's hand.

4.

THAT NIGHT, I was awake when Mom came home from work, which I never was. She constantly reminded us that as soon as she got in the house, she always— and I mean always—came directly down the hall and into our rooms to check on us while we were asleep, and that evening was no different. She enduringly had to make sure her boys were okay the moment she got home. I turned my head when I saw the bedroom door move. She flipped the light on, and I think we both jumped when we saw each other.

"Jeremy?" she asked. "What are you still doing up?"

I adjusted my eyes, squinting at her.

"Can't sleep, Mom," I confessed.

"Aw," she voiced. "Did you say your words?"

I nodded. "I always do. Every night."

She shyly grinned and came towards my bed. "Then what's wrong? Did you have a bad dream?"

Shaking my head, I said, "No, no bad dreams. No dreams at all. Haven't slept yet."

"What are you thinking about then? What's keeping you up?"

I don't know if I actually was tired or it was the fact that I never could lie to my mother without feeling tons of guilt, even at age seven, but the truth just came spilling out.

"Mom, vampires aren't real, right?"

She looked at me stupidly and chuckled. "Vampires? How do you know what vampires are, other than the costumes you've seen at the store, like the one that guy was wearing today. Kids at school say something? That cashier today scare you? He say something bad to you? You see something you shouldn't have on the TV? Your brother?"

God knows I tried to stay silent. I didn't want to get my brother in trouble, and yet I couldn't lie. I pinched my mouth tighter, longer. I needed time.

My mother sighed and looked at me, breaking the silence before I could say anything at all, thankfully. "No, Jeremy. Vampires are not real. Only make-believe."

"How do you know for sure? They look like real people."

"Yes, honey, I know. But listen. I'm a lot older than you, and I've never seen one. And you know why? Because they aren't real. They don't exist. Only in books and movies that are meant to scare you." And just as the light instantly came on in my room, I swear I saw a glow behind my mother's eyes. She knew something right then. She looked towards the doorway for a second before turning back to me. She grinned.

I looked at her, confused. "What, Mom?"

"Nothing, sweets. But you need to trust me. Vampires aren't real, Jeremy. I'm telling you that, and my mom told me that, and one day you'll tell your own children that, too. You'll get over the fear. I promise." She kissed my forehead and told me to try and get some sleep. "I love you. Mom's home. You're safe. Say your words again and try and rest."

I softly smiled. "Love you, too, Mom. Thank you."

"That's what moms do. Protect their kids," she said, hitting the light switch, leaving me in darkness.

Despite my eased mind and the lingering feeling of comfort my mother gave me, I still wasn't entirely convinced, not yet. She could've told me a thousand and one times that vampires weren't real, it wasn't going to change the possibility that they were out there, walking like one of us, disguised. And so, I became superstitious and trusted in the cashier's words. I was trusting him more than my mother. I pulled the blanket over my neck until the bottom of my chin was covered and closed my eyes.

No vampires came that night.

5.

THE FOLLOWING MORNING, I woke up to my mother yelling at Neil. "This is your fault. This is why he wasn't able to sleep last night. He was afraid because of what you guys were watching! Or have been watching when I'm not around." Oh, she was furious. "I trusted you, Neil!" was the last thing I heard before making my way down the hall and to the kitchen toward the voices.

On the kitchen table sat a stack of videotapes.

My heart dropped. She had found them. Neil and I weren't allowed to watch such "garbage," so Neil and his friends had found a spot to hide them in the basement. Apparently, it wasn't a good enough location (worse than the unknown location of the cans of beer still somewhere in the house). I knew then that was why I noticed that light behind her eyes the night before; she knew why I couldn't sleep, why I was all of a sudden educated about vampires, and more, due to the variety of titles on the table.

"You little snot," Neil growled at me. "You told her! You baby!"

"I didn't! I swear!"

"No, Neil," our mother interrupted. "He didn't tell me. I figured it out."

Neil glared at me regardless. I knew then I was cut off from the fun in the basement, if there would ever be such entertainment again, as Neil was about to get grounded for way too long. He slowly walked by me, looked at me with a hate in his eyes, and said: "I'll get you back. I promise. You thought the movies were scary, well..."

I gulped. We were no longer buddies, but he still had to be in the house with me, watch over me, which, at that moment, did scare me more than the movies.

After Neil was back the hall and in his room, Mom asked me: "Are you ready for your birthday party tomorrow? I can't believe you're going to be eight."

I smiled wide.

6.

I DIDN'T SEE Neil at all after Mom left for work. We both stayed in our rooms for most of the day, avoiding one another. I was afraid he was planning something for me. However, I gave him a little credit. When I came out to the kitchen for lunch, I noticed there was a pot still on the stove with a few scoops of ravioli inside. He didn't let me starve, still looking after me, probably fearing our mother more than anything if he neglected me. And yet, I was still wondering what he was up to, how he was going to get me back, as promised.

Mom had called from her second job shortly after eight to check up on us. I told her that Neil and I hadn't talked or seen each other. She sighed into the phone, saying that eventually he'd get over being upset—he'd have to.

"You're not going to watch anything scary with him tonight, are you?"

"No, Mom. Promise. He doesn't even want to be around me. I'm just gonna go to bed soon."

"The sooner you go to bed, the sooner your birthday will come and the party can start."

I snickered into the phone.

"Have a good night, Jeremy. I hope you can fall asleep easier tonight and have sweet dreams. You think you'll be okay?"

"I hope so."

"I know you will. You're about to be a big man."
This time she laughed into the phone. "I love you, honey.
Can you tell your brother to get on the phone now?"

"Love you, too, Mom. See you in the morning."

I put the phone down on the counter, letting the cord
dangle towards the floor. I walked down the hall and yelled
to Neil that Mom was on the phone. I was in my room a
second later.

Neil stomped down the hall as I crawled into bed.
For a moment, I did feel brave; after saying my words, I felt
I didn't need the blanket so high and close to my chin, becoming the bigger man like Mom said. But no, that feeling
didn't last long.

It was an oddly warm autumn night and the window
in my room was still open, letting the comforting, humid
breeze massage the room. I stared at it, battled with myself
not to close it, telling myself it was impossible for a vampire
to come into my room in the middle of the night. Because
they didn't exist. Right? I continued to gaze across the
room, and even though I kept telling myself vampires
weren't real, that Mom was right, I couldn't help but linger
on the possibilities of their existence as I did the night before. Angrily, I threw the blanket off and stood out of bed,
rushing to the window, closing it.

The room almost immediately began to get stuffier,
the breath of the day locked in my room. I put myself in bed
and folded the blanket back over me, pulling it up to my
chin. I was safe, I believed.

7.

SOFT LAUGHTER WAS what made me open my eyes. It was bright in the room, and Neil stood over me. The more I opened my eyes, the more he laughed—and laughed louder.

"What?" I said, feeling the blanket still under my lip. I moved it down quick. "What is it?"

Neil collected himself a bit. "Why do you have your blanket pulled up so far? You look like a scared baby. And why do you have a blanket on at all? It's so suffocating and humid in here." He went to the window.

"No!" I screamed. "Don't open it!"

He looked back, grinning wide.

"What are you so afraid of? Mom said earlier this morning you couldn't sleep 'cause you were afraid.'"

"I'm not afraid," I replied as strong as I could.

"Then you won't care if I do this," Neil said and yanked up on the window.

Fear filled my face and guts.

"Come on. Tell me," Neil insisted. "You can trust me."

I squinted at him.

"I'm not mad anymore," he assured.

"Promise?"

Neil nodded.

"It was that vampire movie. It scared me differently than the others. I think vampires are really, really close to humans. They even look like us. And sometimes act like magicians—and magicians are real!"

"So you think vampires are real?"

"Like…like I know they're not. I know it's just a

movie and not real life, but…what if we just can't tell they are around us since they look like us?"

"And that's why you have the window closed? So vampires won't get in?"

I sighed. "Yes."

Neil then burst into utter laughter, ceasing what sounded like compassion and interest in his voice a moment before. "Oh, please," Neil snorted. "Please, tell me more. What's the story about the blanket then?"

"I'm not going to tell you if you're just going to laugh at me."

Neil came to the side of the bed and drew back his fist. "Tell me or you're getting one of my famous dead legs you hate so much."

Now, my brother was typically a good brother, but we were brothers all the same. And at times, we fought like brothers do. I always lost, though, since I was smaller, younger, but mainly because I'd give up wrestling around with him after he had given me a good, solid punch in the leg. It would stiffen me up and I'd ask for mercy.

"I'm not telling you," I echoed.

Neil didn't say a word, but his fist came flying down, connecting with my right leg.

I yelled and grabbed my thigh, massaging the pain out.

"Jerk!" I screamed.

"Another one's a comin' if you don't tell me." He drew back again.

I caved. "Someone told me that all you have to do to protect yourself from vampires is to pull your blanket up and above your chin so the vampires can't bite you."

Neil fell to the floor in a fit of laughter. He was coughing and choking as he tried to catch his breath. "Oh, man. Oh, man, oh, man, oh, man, this is so great."

I looked at him stupidly, still rubbing my leg.

"You know, I was just gonna come in here and beat on your legs a bit for what you did this morning, but oh, man, this is so, so much better." He began laughing again.

"How? How is this better?"

"Because…you're at an age now where embarrassing things like this will haunt you for a long, long time. My friend, Cam, still hears about how he peed his pants during The Pledge of Allegiance. It happened years ago, back in kindergarten. He still gets made fun of for it. And if I start telling your friends how you're afraid of vampires and think that keeping a blanket over your neck will protect you from them biting you…oh, man," Neil giggled. "I told you I'd get you back."

My heart sank. Would he really embarrass me like that? I knew he was better than that, better than most brothers despite our battles sometimes.

"Don't," I said.

Neil put his head down and giggled, shaking his head. "Oh, man."

"Don't," I repeated.

Neil looked up at me. "Want me to close the window again for you, princess? How 'bout a bottle?"

"Get out! Leave me alone!"

"How 'bout a diaper change?"

"Get out!" I reached to my bedside stand and grabbed a book. I threw it at him.

Neil swatted it away and ran to my side. He drilled

me in the leg, right in the same spot as before. "Don't do that again."

"OUT!"

Neil backed away and finally left, laughing awfully as he did.

I laid there upset, legs throbbing. But more than anything, I was nervous. I sat up and waddled to the window, reclosing it. The blanket then comforted me when I returned.

The sweat came rushing back, but I felt okay.

8.

MY LEG WAS still sore the next morning when I walked down the hall and to the kitchen. As soon as my mother saw me, she blew heavily through a kazoo. There was a party hat already crowning her head. She smiled so wide.

"Happy birthday!" she cheered and came over to me. She hugged me for a long time and then looked in my eyes. "My big man. But big or not, you need one of these." She turned to the table and grabbed a party hat, mounting it on my head like hers. Mom turned back to the table. "Wanna say anything, Neil?"

He looked at me, smiling like a devil, holding my secret. "Happy birthday, buddy."

I tried to smile back at him, tried to trust him.

"Now, I do have good news," Mom began, "but," she sighed and almost started to cry. "I have some bad news, too."

I frowned at her.

"Please, please don't be upset with me."

"I won't, Mom," I assured.

"The grocery store called this morning. Apparently two of the overnight workers quit last night. They said they were desperate for help and asked if I could pull twelve hours this evening. I said it was your birthday, but it didn't seem good enough for them. I'm so, so sorry, honey. We need this job though. I hope you can understand that."

I remember feeling sorry for her. "It's okay," I said. "You're gonna be here for the day though, right?"

"Of course. Actually, I'll be here for the whole thing since I don't have to go into the nursing home today. They were more understanding when I requested off for your birthday party. All the parents today should be picking up the kids by five, and I'm gonna leave around six to go to the store. I should be home around seven tomorrow morning."

"Are Jeremiah and Drew still staying over?" I asked, referring to my two best friends from school. They had stayed over before; their parents trusted both my mother and Neil.

"As far as I know. Your brother will be looking after you guys tonight. Ain't that right?"

Neil looked at us. "Sure am. Promised I would weeks ago. Gonna be fun."

I glared at him. Was he truthful?

"Now, Neil—"

"Mom, stop," Neil interrupted. "I learned my lesson. No bad movies."

Mom smiled at Neil. "Exactly. I'm trusting you, giving you a second chance. Prove me wrong and maybe your own friends can start coming back over sometime soon."

"Deal," Neil said.

"All right," Mom began, "so what's the birthday boy want for breakfast?"

"Make it something good," Neil said. "I'm hungry, too."

9.

BY A QUARTER after five, Jeremiah and Drew were the last of my friends in the house. It had been a great birthday, spent mostly outside since it was still humid, playing games in the yard, eating cake and pizza. Then I was allowed to open the gifts from my friends, mainly cards with small amounts of cash inside. Mom disappeared for a moment, and when she returned to the yard, she had a large, wrapped package in her arms. She handed it to me. Inside was a brand-new gaming console. My friends and I cheered. Neil even helped hook it up to the television in the basement, still being rather nice to me, still keeping his mouth shut about my fear of vampires. We all spent the rest of the birthday celebration in the basement, passing the controller around.

I came out of the basement and walked Mom to the door when she yelled down the steps that she was leaving for work, thanking her repeatedly for the game system, explaining it was the best gift ever.

She smiled. "You're very welcome. Enjoy it. Don't stay up too late playing it. And please, for the love of God, be good for your brother. He seems to have cooled down a bit. I just spoke to him in his room, and he said he wasn't upset with you anymore."

"I hope so. We'll be good, Mom. Promise."

She kissed me on the cheek and walked outside to her car.

I could hear Neil in his room watching television. I hoped he would stay there for the night, just in case he had some prank planned and today was nothing more than a cover up for the big reveal that night.

10.

WHEN I SAY we played that gaming system until we couldn't see straight anymore, I mean just that; we all said how fuzzy the room seemed when we looked away from the television. The clock in the room said 10:22 p.m. after the haze in our eyes settled. Jeremiah yawned first, and then a contagious effect went to each of us.

"You guys just wanna sleep down here tonight?" I asked them.

We normally slept in my room since Neil was usually occupying the basement at night, but that day was my birthday; I had a choice for once.

There were footsteps coming down into the basement.

"Yeah," Drew started, "let's just sleep down here. Play more games if we get up in the middle of the night."

"You all ready for bed or what?" Neil said as he finished coming down the stairs.

"We were thinking about it," I answered.

"Okay, I was just comin' down to see. I saw the

time. How's the gaming going?"

"Really cool," Jeremiah blurted.

Drew and I nodded our heads in agreement.

"Maybe you can show me how to play tomorrow?" Neil said.

I looked at him, studying him. Maybe he really was over being upset with me. He was back to himself, it seemed. I hoped.

"Sure," I said.

Neil smiled. "All right. I'll be right back. You guys are gonna need some more pillows and stuff."

"I call couch," Jeremiah said quickly.

"Chair!" I exclaimed, securing something with a cushion.

"Floor," Drew said slow and almost sad.

"GET A SLEEPING BAG FOR DREW!" I yelled up to Neil.

"Heard ya," he replied from the stairway.

When Neil came back into the basement, we could barely see his face. He had a stack of pillows and blankets. He set them all on the ground in the center of us except for one.

I looked at him.

And he looked back at me, grinning so devilishly wide.

"Here, Jeremy," Neil began, "I made sure to bring down an extra blanket for you. You know, just so you can protect yourself from the vampires."

My heart fucking sank into my feet.

My friends instantly started to laugh at my expense, my embarrassment.

"Yeah," Neil said to Jeremiah and Drew. "Jeremy admitted to me yesterday that he thinks vampires may be real. And he believes that if he keeps his little neck covered with his blankie, no vampires can bite his neck."

Tears started in my eyes. Same with my friends, except they were laughing as hard as my brother was the night before.

"Wittle baby, Jeremy" Neil sang, and then repeated it over and over again until Drew and Jeremiah told him to stop or they'd pee themselves.

I turned away to wipe my eyes.

"Knock it off!" I yelled. "I don't think they're real. I just didn't know for sure."

"Wittle baby, Jeremy," Neil continued.

"Stop it!" I demanded.

Neil balled up the blanket and threw it at me.

I caught it, covering my face.

"Leave us alone," I said into the blanket. "We're going to sleep." Pulling the blanket down, I looked at my friends, who were still smiling at me. "Right?"

They chuckled and nodded their heads, each claiming a pillow and blanket. Drew unzipped the sleeping bag on the floor, and Jeremiah stretched out on the couch.

I glared holy hatred at my brother.

He smiled fiendishly at me. "Told ya I'd get you back. And I'm gonna leave all the windows open and the doors unlocked, too. Let all the vampires in tonight."

My friends were trying to keep it together, covering their mouths.

"SHUTUP!" I screamed.

Neil finally turned away and left. The lights went

off when he hit the switch at the top of the stairs.

The television stayed on, dancing soft light and background voices in the room. Before Jeremiah and Drew fell asleep, they popped a few jokes at me, mainly asking if I needed another blankie or a pacifier, if my neck was completely covered. They'd giggle in the darkness, and I'd tell them to shut the hell up, that I wasn't a baby or afraid. I laid there in silence after I knew they were asleep, fearing what they and my brother would tell kids at school next week. God, I'd be known as a baby, a believer in vampires. But what if I was the one who was right? I still thought it was possible. And so, I quietly said my words before closing my eyes and pulled the blanket up to my chin.

11.

THINKING BACK TO that night, I believe it was the sound of something falling upstairs that woke me up, a blunt thud in the ceiling.

"Jeremiah?" I whispered. "Drew?"

Nothing but silence came from them.

I waited in the dark, listening. For a moment, there was nothing. But then I heard several footsteps creaking above us.

Mom must be home, I thought, assuming, unable to see the clock through the darkness to be sure.

Was it really morning already?

The door to the basement opened, that distinct squeal in the hinges.

Black and anxiety surrounded me.

"Guys?" I peeped.

Still nothing.

The footsteps started. It was then I realized it couldn't have been my mother, unless she had grown two legs and accompanying feet.

There were two people walking downstairs.

I guessed it could've only been my brother and one of his friends that had snuck into the house, ready to pull the ultimate prank on me, the exclamation point to the prior humiliation. I stared at the bottom of the steps. I couldn't see much. The television's bouncing glare only bleached out the shadows of furniture and the stairway.

My body started to shake the closer the footsteps got, louder, despite the blanket still being up at my neck. I gripped my hands around the top of it, holding it close to my mouth in fear.

There was silence again in the room after two tall shadows stopped at the basement floor. This couldn't have been Neil and a friend, not unless they had grown at least a foot since I'd seen them last. I stared at the length of their forms, shaking, lightheaded.

Then they moved, stepping closer to us....

This was when I pinched my eyes shut in fear, letting my other senses take over the experience.

After their footsteps stopped nearby, there were two large gasps that came from my friends' mouths, as if the air had been sucked out of their bodies. I heard several suppressed moans and inhalations, but they were quieter than my whispers to them moments before. Something was prohibiting them from exercising nearly any audible tone, and I didn't believe I would've heard them at all if I wasn't so damn close, listening. And the more I listened, the more I heard a drinking, sucking, gulping noise coming from what I presumed were the foreign entities in the basement.

Gulp, gulp, gulp....

This went on for minutes.

I listened—couldn't escape the sounds. I didn't make a noise, selfish, fearing I was next if I made myself known.

After the gulping noises had stopped, there were two huge sighs of...satisfaction? They panted together.

"One more," one of them exhorted awfully. The voice was deep, but...sharp?

My bladder failed at that moment.

They knew about me....

I kept my eyes closed, continued to keep my hands gripped around the blanket high on my face, now close to the underside of my nose, shivering. At that time, I still didn't know for sure if they were vampires, but stayed in the position I was, locked in the most awful terror I had ever felt.

There was an intense pressure in the air around me after acknowledging the beings were towering above my body on the recliner, one on each side. There was a warmth against either side of my cheek as they came closer to my face, a stench of sourness and mold.

"Let us in," one hissed. "Pull down the sheet."

"Let us in," the other echoed with an even deeper voice. "We know you're still awake."

Two sharp nails then shaped my eyebrows and slowly went down my face. I felt each of their nails slip under the blanket, tugging softly.

"Let us in," they sang.

"No," I reservedly growled.

Each of them snarled, spewing a light mist onto my face.

And still I kept my eyes closed, hands and blanket locked in place.

They yanked harder against the blanket.

"NO!" I barked. "I know how to protect myself from you! I was told how!"

I felt and heard each of them jump back. Instantly, the air around me was less suffocating.

"He knows! He knows the secret," the deeper-voiced creature said. Then they both made some noises I can't exactly explain. Huffs of disbelief? Cries of hurt? I don't know for sure, but they never came back to my side, as if they knew I was stronger with my blanket, with my beliefs, my knowledge.

The last thing they said was: "They're ours now. They come with us."

A parade of footsteps went up the stairs a moment later, then silence found itself back in the basement.

My heart was pounding so hard. Fear kept my eyes closed. The combination of a racing heart and the definition of horror was what I believe made me finally pass out.

12.

MY MOTHER'S VOICE the following morning still haunts me. I shook awake in the basement after hearing it. The television was still on. The chair under me was wet, and there were blankets on the couch and floor. But my friends were missing.

Oh, no. Did that really happen? And it wasn't just a bad dream like before?

"Maybe they're just upstairs? Maybe they scared Mom?"

I jumped out of the chair and raced up the stairs.

I found my mother on her knees in Neil's room, beside his bed.

Jeremiah and Drew were not beside her.

And someone else was in my brother's bed....

I slowly walked closer to the mattress. "Mom. Who, who is that?"

Mom didn't say a word, only syllables in between her crying fit.

But after taking another step, I knew who it was.

The person in Neil's bed was, indeed, Neil. Only he was completely naked, terribly pale, as if his body had been drained of blood. And, if not more awful, he was much shorter, his entire body covered in wrinkles. He was curled up, resembling a baby animal of some kind that didn't survive the birthing. I noticed a small patch of blood on his pillow.

Mom turned to me. "Jesus Christ, Jeremy. What happened last night?"

I started to cry, shaking my head, then my entire body. "Jeremiah and Drew are missing, too."

Her eyes went wide.

"Two people came into the house last night. I saw their shadows when they came down the stairs. But I protected my neck, Mom. I protected my neck like I was told, and they left me alone. It could've only been vampires. I heard them sucking and drinking Jeremiah's and Drew's blood. But I protected my neck when they came to me. I told them I knew how to be safe, and they left. But I think they took them. They said they were going to, and now they're gone."

My mother looked at me blankly and started to laugh, perhaps out of madness or surprise. She didn't believe me. And yet, she did, especially after seeing the several sets of puncture wounds on my brother's neck and various other parts of his shrunken body.

There were small traces of blood on the basement couch and floor where Jeremiah and Drew last rested, but their bodies were never found.

To this day, I still say my words at night and keep the blankets high.

And as far as I know, Mom still does, too, along with my wife and our three kids.

"LONE DINER"

"FORREST, PLEASE. FOR the love of all that is holy, find us somewhere to eat," Gina implored from the passenger's seat, quickly putting her book on her lap, unable to pay attention any longer. "I'm going to start eating these pages."

Forrest smirked at his wife, almost wanting to dare her to eat her book to see if she really was *that* hungry. "Should've gotten up with me and had the hotel breakfast. Or at least had some orange juice. You would've made it home."

Despite her hunger, Gina gagged at the thought of orange juice, rewinding back to the night before when she had far too much contaminated orange juice at her sister's wedding. Her sister lived in northern Idaho, and Forrest and Gina had another two hours west before reaching home where their bed waited for her.

"There," Forrest began, pointing ahead of them, "does that sign say anything about nearby restaurants?"

Gina squinted. "Fast food mainly off the next exit. A handful of them. I don't know how well that's going to go over with me at the moment."

Forrest smirked again.

"But there's a place called 'Mom's Homestyle.' Maybe it's a diner or something? God, I hope I can get the biggest plate of mashed potatoes there. Soak some of this up. Or pancakes. Yes! Pancakes."

"Let's hope it's a diner then," Forrest replied, merging right and off the exit.

They turned left at the light.

The parking lot of Mom's Homestyle was barren aside from the three cars parked out by the dumpsters. The building itself was old and outdated, looking more like an old home than a diner. It appeared there were also apartments upstairs, and a bar attached to the one side of the structure.

"Not sure about the pancakes," Forrest said as they walked to the entrance.

A plaque was nailed beside the door, inscribed with the contractor's name and the year it was built: 1820.

"Wow, two hundred years old," Forrest said. "Probably lots of history in here."

"And hopefully food, too," Gina said, opening the door.

They both stood motionless after walking in, digesting what they had found. The establishment could hold sixty people at most. The floor looked like hotel carpet: dark green with silver filigree, half-worn away at where they stood. The walls were covered in plaid wallpaper—hideous. There was a fireplace against the far wall. And at the table in front of it sat the only other diner: an older woman who appeared to be in her sixties. Her head was down, her hands together, almost looking as though she was praying. She did not have a glass in front of her yet, nor a meal.

The swinging door that led to the kitchen opened. A tall man dressed in a black uniform came out. "Just the two of you?" he asked.

"Yes," Forrest replied.

"Anywhere you like then. I'll go and get our waitress. She'll be right out."

The man went back through the doors.

Forrest and Gina found a small table close to the door, nearly the furthest one away from the lady.

The doors to the kitchen swung open again. A middle-aged female with short, brown hair came through, searching.

"Oh, hello," she said after noticing them. "Were you waiting long? My apologies. I was at the bar tending to the regulars. I'll be running back and forth for another hour. So if you don't see me for a short period of time, that's why. But I won't forget about ya. I promise. What can I get you to drink?" she questioned, laying down two menus.

"Water," Forrest said. "Thank you."

"Same for me," Gina answered.

"Easy enough." The waitress turned and went back through the swinging door.

"Lots and lots of water," Gina chuckled.

"Hope the other lady over there gets taken care of," Forrest said.

"Maybe she came in just before us, and the waitress is getting her drink now or waiting for her food."

Forrest shrugged.

The lady near the fireplace looked up at them. She grinned softly and raised a hand.

They both responded with the same waving gesture.

The lady stood up gingerly, sliding the chair back just far enough so she could stand. She walked silently to a door near the entrance. The bathroom. She opened the door and went in.

"Cute old woman," Forrest said.

Gina nodded, looking over the menu. "I'm out of luck. No pancakes. No breakfast at all. They do have sides of mashed potatoes, though. I'm not entirely doomed."

Forrest smiled and picked up the menu, deciding.

The door to the kitchen reopened and the waitress appeared with two towering glasses of water.

"There ya are," she said, placing each glass before them. "Did I come back too soon? I did, didn't I?"

"Maybe," Gina said.

"Yeah. To be honest, I just picked up the menu. We were talking beforehand. Speaking of which, you know you have another customer, correct?"

The waitress looked at Forrest, befuddled, looking around. "I'm sorry?"

"The older woman that was over at the table by the fireplace." Forrest pointed. "She was sitting there when we walked in. She's in the bathroom now. But we also noticed she didn't have a glass or food in front of her. We figured that maybe she walked in right before us and no one noticed her yet."

"Yeah, she walked into the bathroom about a minute ago," Gina continued.

The waitress turned to the bathroom door and then to the table by the fireplace. She noticed the chair was out from the table further than it should have been, as if someone had truly been there and gotten up. She turned back to the two at the table. "Hmm," she hummed.

"What?" Gina said.

"I'm sorry," the waitress began, "but you're my first diners on this side of the restaurant."

"But we saw her," Forrest corrected.

"I'm sure you did," the waitress replied with a smile, turning away. She went directly to the bathroom door, gripping the knob in her hand.

"No, wait!" Gina yelled. "She's in there."

The waitress opened the door without care and went in, hitting the light. Immediately, a fan turned on....

Forrest and Gina looked at each other, puzzled, realizing they had not heard the fan before.

"She certainly wouldn't have gone in the dark. Right?" Forrest asked his wife.

Gina ignored him.

The waitress peered around the side of the bathroom door, smiling.

"What?" Gina asked, nearly standing.

"The place is haunted, you know?" the waitress said.

Gina fell back in her seat.

Forrest dead-stared the waitress.

"Who you saw was probably the old owner. The baker. Her name was Bev and she died in 1922. We have many walking around here."

Forrest and Gina looked at her, shocked.

"Excuse me one moment, would you?" The waitress said and went back into the bathroom.

Forrest and Gina waited, and waited, and waited, until they were quite concerned. Was the waitress okay in there? They both got up from their chairs and went for the bathroom door.

Forrest knocked.

No answer.

Gina echoed the knock.

Again, no answer.

Forrest opened the door to the bathroom and the only thing inside was a toilet and a fan whirling above.

Confused, Gina went through the swinging door that led to the kitchen.

Forrest followed her.

The man in the black uniform was not there, and none of the appliances were on. In fact, they looked dusty, had not been used for quite some time.

They went through the kitchen and to the bar, where the waitress said she had been serving people. But no one was there, only the two of them and the small whiskey glasses dotting the bar's top.

DISCOVERIES

Vinnie Peachey lives in Pennsylvania with his love,
Kristin, and their pets, Squid and Olive.

Discoveries is his fourth book.

Other Titles by the Author:

Novels:
The Ugly
Tongues

Collections:
Questioning Love and Nature